Lo... When they dance into
be helped ...ve

Alexander Benton is used to getting what he wants. With his wealthy parents MIA most times, he is left to rule Juilliard and half of Manhattan with impunity. He hides his misery behind meaningless sex and condemning behavior.

Augusto Catalan grew up poor. To make a living, he dances at a local gay performance club and survives on the poverty line. His crappy New York apartment and simple life make him happy---except for the death of his lover, his brother being in a war zone and his life-long dream of getting into Juilliard slipping away with each passing day.

When Alex meets Augusto, he knows there is no way this ghetto boy is getting into /his/prestigious school. Then he sees Augusto dance.

MLR Press Authors

Featuring a roll call of some of the best writers of gay erotica and mysteries today!

Derek Adams	Z. Allora	Maura Anderson
Simone Anderson	Victor J. Banis	Laura Baumbach
Helen Beattie	Ally Blue	J.P. Bowie
Barry Brennessel	Nowell Briscoe	Jade Buchanan
James Buchanan	TA Chase	Charlie Cochrane
Karenna Colcroft	Michael G. Cornelius	Jamie Craig
Ethan Day	Diana DeRicci	Vivien Dean
Taylor V. Donovan	S.J. Frost	Kimberly Gardner
Kaje Harper	Alex Ironrod	DC Juris
Jambrea Jo Jones	AC Katt	Thomas Kearnes
Sasha Keegan	Kiernan Kelly	K-lee Klein
Geoffrey Knight	Christopher Koehler	Matthew Lang
J.L. Langley	Vincent Lardo	Cameron Lawton
Anna Lee	Elizabeth Lister	Clare London
William Maltese	Z.A. Maxfield	Timothy McGivney
Kendall McKenna	AKM Miles	Robert Moore
Jet Mykles	N.J. Nielsen	Cherie Noe
Gregory L. Norris	Willa Okati	Erica Pike
Neil S. Plakcy	Rick R. Reed	AJ Rose
Rob Rosen	George Seaton	Riley Shane
Jardonn Smith	DH Starr	Richard Stevenson
Christopher Stone	Liz Strange	Marshall Thornton
Lex Valentine	Haley Walsh	Mia Watts
Lynley Wayne	Missy Welsh	Ryal Woods
Stevie Woods	Sara York	Lance Zarimba
Mark Zubro		

Check out titles, both available and forthcoming, at
www.mlrpress.com

DANCE
FOR ME

ALLISON CASSATTA &
REMMY DUCHENE

mlrpress
www.mlrpress.com

Published by
MLR Press, LLC
3052 Gaines Waterport Rd.
Albion, NY 14411

Visit ManLoveRomance Press, LLC on the Internet:
www.mlrpress.com

Cover Art by Allison Cassatta
Editing by Christie Nelson

Print ISBN #978-1-60820-931-6
Available in ebook format:

Issued 2014

From Allison,

I want to dedicate this book to everyone who has supported me and stood by me through my career as an author. I write books for you. I dance for you.

A special thank you to the staff at MLR for helping bring this book to life.

From Remmy

To my beautiful sista from another motha, Tster – No matter what I do or say you've never given up on me and even those years when you were too scared or shy to say you love me, I knew you did. I heart you so hard.

And to Aster who gave life to Remmy Duchene – I know sometimes life can throw you some curve balls but it's time to knock them out of the park. I love you.

To those who will read this story – I hope it makes you as happy as it made me.

CHAPTER ONE

Augusto sat in the center of his bed, back against the wall, clutching his guitar. It wasn't anything expensive but it was special to him. It once belonged to his father and it was the only thing he owned that he would seriously go back into a burning building for. While strumming at the nickel strings absentmindedly, he stared out the bedroom window at the busy traffic outside. There was nothing worse than where he lived. The only people who lived there were those who couldn't do better. Money was tight everywhere and because of that the whole place was falling apart around them. But the apartment was clean and he had his freedom. His roommate was his best friend and though his philosophy was never to live with a friend, Keith turned out to be amazing support for him.

A barking dog sent a wave of unwanted noise in through the opened window to blend with the beautiful hum of the acoustic guitar. The morbid heat was the only reason he couldn't close the window. It was so hot, each time he breathed it felt like inhaling over an open fire.

When the barking finally got on his nerves, he dropped the guitar to the bed and rushed to the window. He stuck half of his partially nude body out, along with a curled first. "Hey! Asshole! Put a muzzle on that thing!" he shouted. "You're not the only one living here!"

"Up yours!" A voice hollered back.

"I'm so sick and tired of this shit!" he returned. "You either shut that thing up or I will!"

Hauling himself back inside, he slammed the window shut and turned on the two large standing fans sitting on both sides at the foot of the bed. That didn't help—it merely pushed the hot air around then shoved it back into his face. To be honest, the bedroom was the coolest part of the apartment. The other rooms were worse since they faced the side that soaked in the sun all day. Augusto could scarcely breathe, so he put the guitar on his bed and exited the bedroom.

Not sure what he was going to do with himself, he sucked air into his lungs through his mouth, because inhaling through his nose caused a burning sensation. He wandered into the kitchen and grabbed some ice water from the fridge. Instead of closing it, he stood before the open icebox with his bare back to it. Writhing as the cool air flowed over his skin, he couldn't help likening the pleasure to a lover's touch. The cold on his body was heaven. He couldn't stand there forever but it would help for a little bit. When he was forced to close the door because of thoughts of wasting electricity, Augusto did so only after snagging a tray of ice cubes from the freezer. He lay on his back on the floor and dragged one cube to its death across his abs then up his neck. When it melted completely, he reached for another, tracing it slowly down his body, then between his thighs.

The relief ended too quickly and soon the cubes were gone. His roommate found him an hour later on the same wet patch on the floor.

"Whoa, Gus, you okay, man?" Keith asked, kneeling beside him. "Why are you lying on the floor? And why in Sam Hill is it so damn hot in here?"

"The AC is out *again* and they don't know when it'll be fixed."

"Um…why is the floor wet?"

"Trying to stay cool—ice cubes." Saying full sentences took too much out of him.

"Right…Come on. Get dressed. We'll go down to the diner on the corner and just sit there. It'll be cool and give us a little relief for a bit."

"But we have to buy something—I need to get paid first. I don't think we should be spending extra money right now."

"It's not going to break the bank, Gus. We just have to buy a Slurpee or something." Keith made a face. "Would you put some pants on? It's weird when I come home and you're walking around half-naked."

Keith hurried off down the short hall to his room, saying something about Augusto going out and auditioning for stuff rather than staying at home withering away. But Augusto *had* been trying to become a dancer—after four hundred and eighty-seven auditions, three hundred and ninety-two callbacks and three hundred and ninety-two rejections, he was done. He was drained and couldn't do it anymore.

Augusto rolled over and curled his body in the wet spot as best he could.

"Have you given any thought to Julliard? And why aren't you wearing pants?"

"You can't just audition for Julliard, Keith."

"Why not?" Keith countered.

He twitched a little and took a breath. "I'm not auditioning for Julliard. If for some reason I get in, how in the hell am I going to pay for it? I can barely pay rent. I haven't bought new clothes in four years. I couldn't take another heartbreak—hell, that one would kill me."

"Oh, you're being melodramatic."

Augusto heard Keith's footsteps disappearing down the hall again and soon they were back and a pile of clothes was chucked at his head. He grunted and reluctantly left his perfectly cool spot to haul them on. He would go to the stinking diner—if only to get Keith to shut the hell up about the damn audition. It'd been a while since he had a day off. He didn't want to spend it in their local haunt, watching people who had their dreams come true, going about their day as if nothing else mattered but them.

He was right—sitting in the diner was torture. The AC was magnificent, but being there translated to a whole other kind of unease. "They know, you know?" Augusto said to his best friend. "They know I don't amount to anything."

"And whose fault is that?" Keith snapped. "You're the one choosing to give up. Shit, Gus! Do you know what I would do for your talent? You can dance better than most of these fools and you're just going to throw that away."

"Don't stop there. Tell me how you really feel!"

Keith pushed the plate of fries he'd been shoving into his mouth to the side and leaned in like he was about to impart the meaning of life. He pointed an accusatory finger at Augusto. "When you dance, it's like the world disappears and you're in this zone. None of these zombies have that. Man, you're free on that stage. There's no worry about rent, or money or being single—none of that seems to matter when you're dancing. So a few people didn't see it. Who gives a flying fuck? Go out there and do it again and again and again until something happens. Life is trial and error and just because some brain dead zombies didn't know a good thing if it reached up and bit them on the ass, doesn't mean you should let that dictate your life."

"It's not that easy."

"Of course it is. Do you think me working full-time and going to school full-time is easy? Sometimes, I'm so tired I want to crazy glue my eyelids open. I work mad hours and there's forty bucks in my account. But you know what? I keep telling myself it's not forever. That one day, I'm going to be walking those streets in blue—with a badge on my chest I can be proud of. What are you going to do?"

"I'm doing it, man," Augusto eased back in the uncomfortable chair. "I'm living the fucking dream."

Keith rolled his eyes. "See? I can't talk to you when you get like this."

"Like what?"

"Being a giant asshole."

"I'm sorry," Augusto apologized. "I'm just tired of failing."

"Then stop failing. If I can make it into the academy, you can do anything. Just try again."

Augusto reached for some of Keith's fries and chewed thoughtfully. The simple truth, he still didn't like the idea of putting himself out there. He wasn't sure his heart could take another rejection.

CHAPTER TWO

"You're overdoing it again," Carolynne warned as she rotated Alex's inflamed foot. He winced when she clamped one hand down over the back of his ankle and the other over the tips of his toes. "You can't practice twenty-four-seven."

"I haven't been," Alex snapped. With a groan, he fell back on his bed and closed his eyes. She continued to slowly turn his foot while his dreams slid down the drain.

He and Carolynne had been rehearsing for the parts of Franz and Swanhilda in the sophomore production of Coppelia. It was something the students had been doing for a long time and the shows were always performed in front of sick and dying children from various hospitals around New York. Alex supposed it made the more pompous, elitist students feel better about themselves.

"Alexander Benton," Carolynne screeched. "Are you even listening to me?"

"Truthfully?" No, he wasn't. He was rather enjoying the plush, silky surface of his huge bed. "What were you saying again?"

Rolling her eyes, Carolynne rounded her shoulders as she shoved his swollen foot away from her lap. The sudden thrust pushed a spike of pain up through his calf, to his thigh and into his gut. Alex supposed he deserved that. He had, after all, been slave-driving her into four hour a day practices, and that was after a full schedule at Julliard.

Alex rolled onto his side, curling his legs behind him and cradling his head to his plush pillow. He watched her half-stomp, half-hobble across the room, and honestly, he sort of felt bad about being such a pushy partner…sort of.

"When you go back to your place," he said softly, "will you tell Kenneth to come see me? Please?"

She glared at him for a long, quiet moment, the *how-dare-you* written in the arch of her brow and pinch of her lips. He knew that expression well. In fact, it was the very thing that led to them being friends…after Alex had explained they would be unstoppable if they stopped trying to beat each other for the limelight and joined forces instead.

"Please?" Alex begged again, voice lilting as he gave Carolynne a look she'd always said she couldn't say no to.

"Fine! But I swear to God, if you stay up all night screwing your brains out, I don't want to hear a single word about it when tomorrow's practice sucks royally for you."

"You mean *if* I can dance tomorrow." He glanced down at his currently incapacitated foot. "Maybe Kenny can heal me. You know…sexual healing. They wrote a song about it." He snickered wickedly. Carolynne only rolled her eyes again.

As soon as he heard the door slam behind her, he lay back against his bed again and closed his eyes. Admittedly, he felt rather pathetic for trying to hang on to Kenneth McNamara the way he did, but he couldn't help it. Kenneth had that edgy, gritty, in-your-face bad boy thing Alex loved so much. Though why he craved a blue-collar cutie like Kenneth, why he had a proclivity for men more likely to go to jail than make it on the big stage was beyond him. Maybe it was their sense of adventure and intrigue, the very taboo nature of their being. Maybe it was simply to piss off his mommy and daddy.

The longer time dragged on, the more he doubted Carolynne had done as he'd asked, or maybe Kenneth had finally had enough of him. He wasn't sure. He only knew Kenneth should've been there by now. The siblings lived on the second floor of the building. He lived on the fourth. Half of Julliard took up the rest.

Damn it, Kenny where the hell are you?

"Guess I'm being stood up," Alex muttered as he shoved up from the bed. He only dared to put his weight down on his left foot. The right hurt too badly to even touch. Then he hobbled out of his bedroom and into the kitchen he rarely used.

He grabbed a bottle of water from fridge, then sank down onto a barstool parked on the backside of the island, utterly bored and growing more pissed off as the minutes moved on. If Kenneth didn't hurry, Alex would seriously consider replacing his boy toy with a more considerate model. But God, that man could sing. He sounded like an angel, even when they screwed and Kenny bellowed Alex's name toward the ceiling. His voice sounded just as magical as a perfectly tuned piano or grand golden harp. It was almost enough to make Alex swoon. Almost.

Tap. Tap. Tap. Oh, Alex knew that light rapping of knuckles well. His sexy bad boy had come to him, just as he'd summoned. The thought of that gorgeously muscled body wrapping around his backside elicited an excited shiver.

"Coming," he called. The one word trailed into a purr.

Wincing as he pressed the wrong foot to the floor, he gripped the granite countertop tightly and held on so he could shift his weight from his swollen appendage. He hobbled over to the door, shedding his shirt before answering his sexy gentleman caller. He had on nothing but the dance tights he'd worn to school. Courtesy would've been cleaning the sweat from his body before venturing off into a salacious tryst with the singer extraordinaire, but hindsight being what it was, it left him with the possibility of being nailed against the tiled wall of his oversized shower by a man strong enough to lift him from his feet.

He ran his hands down his slender frame. There was enough sweat left to give his slight tan a healthy sheen, enough to look sexy in the dim light of his apartment too. Then he raked his fingers through his short dark hair. It was tousled from dancing, but a little extra mess never hurt any good, modern coiffure.

Alex wrenched the door open. "Well, hello there."

Kenneth stood there with his hands buried deep in the pockets of his lightly faded jeans, tawny chin-length locks of silken hair hanging around his ruggedly handsome face. A light blue T-shirt hugged the glorious mounds of his toned chest. Just seeing him made Alex imagine running his tongue around each pec, each nipple, down the lines of Kenny's immaculate six-pack, down the V pointing down to Kenny's sweet spot, down…

Kenneth cleared his throat.

"Sorry, I was ogling your goodies," Alex admitted with a devious smirk.

Kenneth's stare bounced around the hallway, obviously looking to see if anyone had heard what Alex had said. If his luscious bad boy had one flaw, it was that he hadn't come out of the closet to anyone but Carolynne yet, and save for their late night interludes in Alex's apartment, the two of them never crossed paths. Alex was his dirty little secret. Not that Alex minded one bit.

"Can I, um…come in or something?" Kenny nervously asked.

Without saying a word, Alex moved from the doorway.

Instead of guiding Kenny to the bedroom, or the couch, or the kitchen counter where their heated rendezvous normally commenced, Alex started toward the bathroom, not bothering to look back to see if Kenny was keeping up. If his darling Kenneth knew what was best for him, he would be right behind Alex and definitely not questioning what Alex had in store for him.

Alex simply said, "Strip," as he reached inside the bathroom and turned the light on.

Without turning around, he knew Kenny had begun doing as he'd been told. The whine of his zipper sliding down told the tale. The sound made Alex smile, but not in a way Kenny could see because that would give too much of his enjoyment away. Theirs was a relationship where Kenneth had to be kept on his toes, never knowing if Alex truly liked him or just wanted to fuck him. Alex kept his pleasure with Kenny buried deep inside, only allowing it to come through during those moments of orgasm when no man in the throes of bliss would have the will to control themselves.

As he reached into the shower to start the water warming, he heard the thud of Kenny's shoe hitting the floor. Then the other one. When he turned back around, he found his part-time lover standing in the doorway in nothing but his birthday suit. Alex smirked. His mouth watered and his cock twitched with joy. The leotards caressed his tightening sac.

"Get in the shower," he demanded as he hooked his fingers around the waistband of his dance tights. The stretchy fabric rolled as he pulled the getup away from his body, his hardening shaft springing free with delight. "Sing me a song while I fetch a condom, would you, lover?"

And just like that, his angel started to sing.

CHAPTER THREE

The line outside Santo's stretched down the block. It usually happened that way—especially on performance nights. Everyone who was anyone in the visible minorities of New York wanted to get on the list. Even those not on the list lined up early, hoping to be allowed in. Santo's only turned people away when it reached capacity and not a second before. The club wasn't exactly mainstream, but it didn't fit the underground definition either. The working class went there—the dancers who moved to the beat and not classical training filled every nook and cranny of the place. Their live dance shows and killer DJs from around the world brought people in from all over the state, sometimes the country.

Augusto was one of their dancers. It'd taken the hook up with the owner's son, Kemar, to get him the gig and he only accepted it because he thought it would be by Kemar's side. Sadly, a year later Kemar died. Kemar's father, Luther, who had taken a liking to the Augusto, kept him on.

Augusto hauled in some breaths and stepped from the semi-crowded train. With skill and familiarity, he navigated the underground promenades, jogged up some stairs instead of taking the escalator and exited the train station. He wrapped his infinity scarf around his neck then pulled the excess over his head like a hood. After sticking his earbuds into his ears and cranking up the music, Augusto stuck his hands deeply into his pockets and set out on the two-block walk to the club. His only stop was a nearby coffee shop to grab a cup of dark coffee with nothing in it. Kemar had always asked how he could drink that crap but Augusto always had a comeback for the question.

"What can I say, Kemar? I like my coffee like I like my men—strong and dark."

The memory made him laugh just as he arrived at Santo's and eased his way past the line to the back of the building. At the door he removed the hood, showing the guard his face.

"You really should stop wearing that thing, especially in this heat," Patrick said, bumping fists with Augusto.

"You know me," Augusto tossed over his shoulder. "Always tall, dark and mysterious."

Patrick laughed and he continued on his way to do his regular routine. Augusto didn't take the stage with his group for another hour but he poked his head out to see what the dance floor looked like. It still wasn't as crowded as it would get. The DJ spun some random tracks but none of the good stuff yet so he hurried into the changing room he shared with the other dancers.

The room was like a train ride to Hades. The noise always made Augusto want to snap, and with Keith riding his ass about the upcoming auditions for Julliard, his temper was a lot shorter than it usually was by the time he got into the room. Still, he made his way in and chucked his bag on his chair. A few dancers darted in, doing the same dance they always did around each other before hurrying out again. He stared at his reflection in the mirror and his heart did a strange leap. It was the same feeling he got whenever he was irritated with something.

Upon closer inspection, his brown eyes seemed dead and he should really think about shaving. Rubbing a hand over the hair on his face, Augusto turned from his reflection's eyes, moved his bag from his seat and flopped into it.

"You made it!" Chet Mullings cheered.

Chet had auditioned one too many times for Julliard and had all but given up on ever making something of himself. It seemed as if a part of his soul was taken each time they brought down that heavy fist of rejection. Chet became the kind of burnout dancer Augusto felt like. Just the mention of Julliard got Chet into a tizzy of a *don't get me started* conversation which he'd totally get started on. Chet was bitter.

"Yeah barely. The heat out there is murder."

Chet laughed. "Still you wear that scarf."

"Yeah. It keeps the sun off my skin."

"Yeah." Chet chuckled. "You're fragile."

Augusto rolled his eyes but laughed. He and Chet had become somewhat friends over the years and he wanted to ask Chet about Julliard.

"Well, I'm glad you're here." Chet tilted his head. "Since our routines are together. It would suck having to do it alone."

Augusto laughed. "That would have been something to see," he joked. "All right let me get changed and we can knock out some rehearsals before we have to hit the stage."

His friend nodded and turned to peer at his reflection in the mirror. Augusto took the time to slip from his track pants into the loosely fitted jeans they'd set out for him as well as a tank top and a pair of brand new running shoes. He laced them up, then paced around the room to get a feel for them. He disliked new shoes. They pinched and bunched in all the wrong places.

"Ready?" Chet questioned.

"In a second," Augusto replied.

He dug into his bag for a stick of gum like he always did and once he gave it a few chews, he spat it in the garbage. Taking a breath, he rubbed his palms against his thighs, tucked his cross pendant into his shirt against his flesh then faced Chet. "Now I'm ready."

They made their way through a few run-throughs of some of their routines and by the time they were ready to breach the stage, Augusto's nerves disappeared.

Game on.

Hitting the stage that night was no different than every other night. The crowd was pumped and everyone cheered. They were so loud he could hardly hear the music. He had to put in his earpiece. The thing felt so uncomfortable he never liked using it. Still, he went through his routine, getting the club hyped, pouring himself into every move. When the show drew to a close, he was exhausted and the pressure of every decision he still had to make swarmed in on him.

"You wanna go to the after-party?" Chet questioned when they sat down to get dressed.

Augusto shook his head. "Nah, I want to get some sleep tonight."

"You sick or something?" Chest clamped his palm over Augusto's forehead.

"Something like that. I'm just not feeling well since the heat wave hit us. The dancing took something out of me so I need to recuperate."

"Not even a drink?"

"Sorry man. Rain check?"

Chet nodded and after a quick hug, left him alone to his thoughts. The other dancers had long since gone and though Augusto wanted nothing more than to stop for a drink, he really wasn't feeling up for a party.

Getting to the apartment from Santo's was a bit of a walk after being on stage all night. Normally the train would be the best way to go, especially so late, but he would have to take two trains for that. He went the long way, thinking the night air would do him good. Probably even knock him out so he could sleep. By the time he got home, endured the elevator ride all the way to his floor and burst into the unit, he was physically exhausted. Thankfully, the air conditioner greeted him at full blast. With that worry out of the way, his first order of business was to raid the kitchen. On the counter he found a plate covered with a note that simply said *Gus* on it. A smile traced his lips as he pulled the cover off to the scent and view of Roti stuffed with curried chicken.

Keith was an awesome roommate. The man was a culinary genius!

Augusto dropped the plate in the microwave and had his finger poised to set the timer when he heard his name.

"In the kitchen, Keith."

He went ahead and started the microwave then turned in time to see Keith enter the room. Keith looked as though he'd been sleeping on the same side all night, leaving pillow welts on his cheek. Augusto laughed. "Thanks for dinner."

"I figured you wouldn't eat anything because you don't take care of yourself."

"We've had this argument." Augusto sighed.

"Yes, but you still don't take care of yourself."

Augusto shrugged. "I've been thinking about Julliard."

Keith grabbed a bottle of water but didn't reply until after he'd wrung the cap off, downed half the contents and recorked the bottle. "And?"

To Augusto that long of a pause deserved something a little more than *and* as a reply. He grabbed a fork and peered into the microwave to see his plate turning and *turning*. "I'll do it."

"You're not just saying that, are you?"

"No." The microwave beeped then went silent. "I figure I don't want to be another Chet. In a few years he'll be too old for anything, too old for working at Santo's, too old period. And what does he have to fall back on? Nothing at all. I don't want to be like that. I need to have something to fall back on. I have some money saved up and Luther said he'd help me out with a scholarship-like-thing. You'll have a badge and can teach at the academy when you're too old to chase a bad guy…"

"Gus…"

"No. I don't want to be a failure."

"You won't be. This Julliard thing is just something you can try. If that doesn't work there are other things but at least you can say you tried."

"I don't want to be a failure," Augusto repeated softer this time.

Keith hugged him tightly. "You won't be. I won't let you. And you can never be like Chet. He's not as pretty as you."

Despite his depression and the overwhelming feeling of what was about to happen, he laughed at Keith's joke. "Thanks, Kay."

Keith released him and picked up his water bottle. "You're welcome. Now, grab dinner and come watch *Big Eden* with me."

CHAPTER FOUR

"Pirouette. Pirouette. Pirouette. Pirouette," their instructor went on, pointedly clapping her hands together as she barked at her students. Each one did as they were told. Some managed to stay on balance. Some happened to fall out of line.

Poor freshman, Alex thought, head cocked to the side, lean body propped against the wall. They all needed to go through this though, even the good ones. It built stamina. It taught those big-eyed, big-dreaming children what the real world of ballet was like. It was a brutal, cut-throat rat-race of a gig, and the weak would never, ever survive.

"Stop smirking," Carolynne whispered. "You look like an arrogant ass."

"I *am* an arrogant ass," Alex quietly chided.

"Touché."

Sighing, Alex crossed his arms over his chest. He wanted so badly to shift his weight off his one good foot, but the other hadn't stopped hurting yet and he feared three days without practice would put him too far behind to even dare to audition for the part of Franz as he'd planned. Sure, it wasn't the grand stage at Julliard, performing for proud parents and trustees, but it was the one volunteer gig he looked forward to. Even someone as shallow as he could sympathize with the strife of a sick child, appreciate the joy on their faces when people performed *just* for them.

"Stop that," Carolynne said, pushing her thumb up and down his wrinkled brow. "That pensive look is going to age you. You're too beautiful to look old."

"I didn't realize I was doing anything."

"Well, you were." She paused, glancing out over the freshman. A thoughtful expression crossed her face. "Are you going to watch the auditions this afternoon? They're trying to fill the last two freshman spots."

"I don't know. Who really cares about a bunch of wannabe dancers?"

"You do," she said. Alex turned to her and caught her smirking. "Oh, c'mon, you know you do. Might see something in the crop you like."

"I highly doubt that. Besides, I'm kind of seeing—"

"My brother. Yes, I'm *very* aware."

"Oh?" He gave her a questioning look. "Has Kenny been talking about me?"

"Talking? Um, no, but I know what goes on. I'm not stupid."

"You know we're not serious, right?"

"Yes." Carolynne seemed so disappointed. "I don't need either of you to tell me that."

"We're happy with what we have. I give him what he wants. He satisfies all of mine. It works for us."

"Well, one can hope."

Alex turned back in time to catch another freshman biting the dust. The girl collapsed right in the middle of her classmates, spinning into a round of fouetté en tournants all around her. Alex might've have quietly laughed to himself had he not remembered falling out just like that on Friday night, leading to his swollen foot and his seriously questionable chance of performing in Coppelia.

With that last heartbreaking thought, he shook his head and tried to go back to imagining Kenny again—the way that lyrical genius rode him hard from behind as they'd stood in Alex's shower, the way his lover always obeyed his every command, the way Kenny made him come harder than anyone had in a long time. Alex wasn't in love with Kenny as a person. The man seriously had no depth. He was a handsome body and a beautiful voice, a gifted poet and damn fine lover, but beyond that, Kenny really didn't offer much. He had that whole bad boy thing going for him, but frankly, he bored the hell out of Alex almost as much as he physically excited him.

"So, about those auditions," Alex said, leaning a little closer to Carolynne. "If we go now, we can probably sneak in without getting caught."

"Everyone knows the sophomores watch the auditions. They never kick anyone out."

"Unless one instructor has a stick up their ass." Alex nodded toward said instructor who was currently cursing a boy for his horrible form and how he looked like a limp noodle whipping around mid-seizure.

Ouch.

They both hissed as they ducked out of the room. They'd been waiting for the class to let out since they'd made an arrangement to use that space to practice for the show. The particular instructor who was berating that poor, trembling boy just so happened to love Alex and Carolynne, had said many times they were both destined for stardom, turning them into two of the most elite dancers in the school. Only problem for Alex was, he had nothing beyond ballet, which seriously limited him on the kind of gigs he'd be able to get.

Carolynne reached down and grabbed his hand. Her touch pulled his attention away from the line of glass windows overlooking New York City. Obviously, she could tell he was more than a bit miffed about his foot. He probably shouldn't have been on it, but lying around the apartment while he withered away just wasn't his style. He would've gone stir crazy if he had to spend another twenty-four hours staring at the same four walls.

"Cheer up, sweetie," she said, offering her side for him to lean against.

He curled his arm around her shoulders and let her hold his slightly larger frame just so he could take the weight off his foot.

"Thank you," he said. "I swear I'll prop it up when we get down to the auditorium."

"And you'll put ice on it when you get home," she added for

him.

Alex laughed. "Of course I will."

"No sex. I'm not kidding. If I have to tie Kenny to the bed, I will."

"Kinky."

She playfully slapped his arm, which only made him laugh harder.

They arrived at the auditorium and Alex reached out to open the door. He held it as Carolynne made her way in first. The lights were low, save for four bright spotlights across the center of the stage. A table setup in front where the orchestra would've been was occupied by six very displeased administrators—each being the heads of their respective departments, as well as the dean of admissions and one student advisor taking notes.

The first candidate was a beautiful, slender woman with the longest legs Alex had ever seen. She kept her shoulders perfectly squared and her chin slightly lifted. From all the way in the back of the room, she looked gorgeous, but the right makeup and right lighting had a way of turning even the ugliest duckling into a swan. Alex put little faith in what his eyes saw at the moment. He would hold his judgment until he saw her moves.

"Right here," Carolynne whispered, indicating two seats all the way in the back of the room, not far from where a few of their classmates sat.

It was so dark none of the staff would see them, even if the six upfront knew they were sitting back there. No one would say anything about it as long as they behaved themselves, kept quiet and respected the potentials pouring their hearts into their moves. Alex could do that. He could bite his tongue and quietly watch those people try to achieve their dreams. After all, he'd been up there doing the same at one point.

He sat down beside Carolynne and popped his foot up on the chair in front of him, then steepled his arms, locking his hands beneath his chin. His elbows rested on each armrest. He watched the first dancer go through her routine, unimpressed with what he saw. She looked like any other seasoned ballerina, every other starlet with big dreams and the kind of money it took to make those dreams happen. Again, unimpressive.

"Thank you, Ms. Grayson," one of the instructors said. She bowed low from the hips then quickly exited the stage. "Mr. Augusto Catalan."

Alex watched with curiosity, waiting to see the person belonging to such a wonderfully exotic name. Latino dancers were always beautiful. It was one of those golden rules, but Alex never really had a thing for gorgeous Latino dancers. They were always too prissy, too sensitive and too needy. Alex had never met one who appealed to the side of him that craved mystery, intrigue and danger. For all the exotic, they always lacked the bad boy image he loved so much.

Then Augusto Catalan took the stage with his loose denims and his solid black tank top, his obviously muscled chest, tan skin and beautiful black hair. He definitely had Alex's attention.

"This should be interesting," Alex said, more to himself than his friend sitting beside him. "Looks like the hood emptied out right in the middle of Lincoln Center."

Carolynne snickered. A few glaring faces turned their way, causing Carolynne to clamp her hand down over her big mouth. Alex only grinned wickedly. While he might've been cracking jokes, he couldn't help but find himself completely mesmerized by the man standing center stage.

CHAPTER FIVE

Augusto wasn't really sure why he allowed Chet's failures to push him into this. He'd never been one to cave under peer pressure or jealousy. But when they called his name, he couldn't turn back. Augusto did all he could do—took a deep breath, ensured his pants were on right and walked onto the stage as if he had all the courage in the world. He figured once he began dancing, he'd be all right since it always made him feel as if he could do anything. Looking down from the stage at the people he had to audition for, he wondered if any of them would understand what he was doing. They looked wealthy, with a pickle up their asses and probably would simply scoff at him. It took everything inside him not to turn and run off the stage. The urge to rub his hands against his thighs surged through him. He often did that when nerves threatened to get the better of him. In those times, his hands got too sweaty.

Standing before these people terrified him. Again he felt like running, and for the first time since the train ride to the school, he was glad Keith hadn't accompanied him. He never wanted Keith to see him as a coward. Anyone else, he didn't care but it would break him if his best friend saw him run. It was strange. Augusto could handle Keith calling him a failure or a loser, but never a coward. Just that thought alone pushed his feet closer and closer to the microphone at the edge of the stage. It seemed to take forever to reach, for the stage was enormous—bigger than the one at Santo's. If he wanted to be honest with himself, it was the biggest stage he'd ever been on and he prayed that it wouldn't be the last time.

"Hello." He managed to say the one word without his voice breaking. It was customary to introduce himself but he didn't trust himself to speak again. Luck was never his best attribute and he knew if he even thought of saying anything else, his voice would crack.

"Mr. Catalan. Did you give your music to the audio personnel?" The woman asking sat upright, dressed in a grey suit with her hair tied back too tight for her slender face.

"Yes, ma'am," he replied.

"Very well. Let's see what you have for us."

Nodding, Augusto froze for a brief moment before gathering himself and taking a step back. Someone removed the microphone stand from the stage and he found his center in the middle of it. He rooted himself, trying to make the people sitting before him disappear as he waited for the music. His heart, which had been racing out of control, slowed and he slipped into that zone he always fell into just before hitting the stage at Santo's. He imagined all the people in the room to be clubgoers who were simply there for a good time.

This is not a life or death situation, Gus.

Once the music began, he allowed his body to fall into the well-practiced first moves. The second set took him downstage, back arched, face up to the sky.

The moves came to him as though he was born to them, but this time it was different. This time the dance meant something. Keith's words kept going through his head.

Think about it, Gus. You're not doing this for them. It's all about you. Own that stage.

But he doubted these prissy people knew hip-hop. There was nothing he could do about that. He had to be himself and hip-hop, Krump was all him. It was easy to just let the music take him where it wanted, gliding across the stage. He could feel it, every single beat, every change in the song and the vibrations it caused. He took the vibrations, allowed them to bounce off his heart and pulsate through his veins like the very blood keeping him alive. The rhythm used him in the same ways it always did, but for some reason this time felt better, freer. The routine carried him through hints of ballet spinning on the tip of his toes like Michael Jackson, then into slight hints of contemporary.

He was meant to be on that stage and suddenly he knew it.

But he couldn't become too confident. Though he might not have the classic training, hip-hop was a little bit of everything.

When the music stopped at the end of his routine, his chest heaved but it was for a whole other reason. It was exhilaration. Adrenaline flowed through him like a river, leaving him feeling as though he could take on the world. Now his future depended on a few people who probably didn't know what in the world he'd just done.

"Thank you, Mr. Catalan," the woman said. "Please wait in the hall."

Augusto's nervousness returned and he nodded then exited the stage. Somehow he managed not to run off like they'd set his pants on fire. He walked off the same way he came in, hopefully masking any sign of nervousness he was feeling. Then again he wasn't a very good actor so he probably failed miserably. Augusto took a moment to grab his bag before hurrying out the side door leading to the waiting area.

He couldn't stay in the hall with all the other possible students. They were pacing back and forth, muttering to themselves and pantomiming dance moves as they went. Augusto knew how they felt and that sheer fright that hinged on the lines of madness was contagious. Walking through the hall was like maneuvering through rush hour traffic. He eased his way through the writhing bodies, the ballet dancers *en pointe*, then he hurried through a lobby area that looked like something from *Star Wars*. Finally free of the crowd, he all but burst out of the glass doors. He bent over, gasping for air like someone had been holding his nostrils shut.

When he could hold it together, somewhat, he turned and stared up at the building. It resembled a regular business building except the front moniker stood proud in glass with white lettering. To his right, the breakable windows were used as displays for advertisements for the school and to showcase past students who'd made something of themselves after graduating. There were two large flower tubs, one to either side of the entrance and just steps away, close to the curb, was a spot to leave bikes.

Just standing before the building he felt small, insignificant.

He needed his fix of music—something to clear his head. Dragging his eyes from the building, he rooted around in the bag for his iPod and stuffed the earbuds into his ears. He found a small wall and sat, bopping his head to *Smooth Criminal* by Michael Jackson.

"Interesting moves, rookie," a voice said from beside him. Augusto raised his head and found an atypical brown-haired, blue-eyed, preppy white boy staring at him like he didn't belong there and didn't have a chance in hell of getting in. The girl behind him smirked. "Learn that in the barrio?"

Augusto took a breath and pulled an earbud from his ear to spare the guy a glance. "Funny. You're a regular Robin Williams."

"Watch it, macho boy. You don't know who you're talking to. I can make your life here hell, presuming you've got what it takes to get in." White boy arched his brow, arms crossed over his chest. A smirk contorted what might've been handsome features if the guy wasn't such an asshole. "From what I saw on that stage, you don't have a chance in hell."

Augusto eyed the guy with contempt but said nothing for a moment. He tilted his head, wondering what game this guy was trying to play. "We'll just have to see about that, won't we? As for making my life hell here." August took a breath and pushed his shoulders back nonchalantly. "Oh, *so* scared."

"You should be. You really should be." The guy smirked again and started stalking away, the quiet girl behind him in tow. He stopped once, looked back and said, "Maybe we'll both get lucky and I won't see you around." And without giving Augusto a chance to argue, the guy continued down the walkway then disappeared through a set of glass double doors leading back into the school.

"Do you know who that was?" The smoking dancer to his left questioned as Augusto was about to slip the earbud back in his ear.

"I should care because?" Augusto questioned.

"That's Alexander Benton," the shy male replied. His hand shook as he pulled the cigarette to his lips for another unhealthy drag. "You should care. If you do get in he can make your life miserable. He's like—God around here."

"I'll let you know when I give a damn," Augusto said. "And by the way—as a dancer, you shouldn't be smoking." He dragged the cigarette from the dancer's hand and hopped from the wall, dropping the lit cigarette to the ground.

"Hey!"

Augusto didn't answer. He merely headed back inside where it was cool to await whatever came next.

CHAPTER SIX

"That kid has a thing or two to learn if he thinks he's going to make it here," Alex said, chuckling softly as he and Carolynne made their way through the school, toward the back lot where the shuttle from Lincoln Center would carry them the few blocks over to the apartment building they shared.

Had it not been for the busted foot, Alex might've just walked. The exercise did his body good anyway, kept his limbs nice and limber, his body strong and toned. But as it stood right now, all the walking around the school had already done him in.

The shuttle ride back to the apartment wasn't horrible, though by the end of it, his foot and ankle were throbbing so hard he could feel the pain in his temples. It made his head ache and his vision blur. When he finally stood up again, he could almost feel the blood rushing down to the lower half of his body.

"You're pale," Carolynne said as she hooked her arm around his waist.

"I think I overdid it today," he huffed as he settled into her side. "It hurts worse than it did Friday."

"Okay, that's it. No more walking around for you. Doc's orders. I'm going to get you somewhere and prop that leg up, and you're not to move until all the swelling is gone. Got it?"

"Will you send Kenny over to be my wet nurse?" Alex teased.

Carolynne rolled her eyes. "No. I won't. And he won't be coming up to see you until you're better."

"Well, damn."

They climbed into the elevator and Alex leaned against the wall, gripping the rail so tightly his knuckles turned white. With the blood rushing down to his swollen foot, the pounding in his shoe hurt so bad it made his head swim. He feared something bad had happened, something so awful it might prevent him from dancing in Coppelia even if he did somehow manage to get the part.

"Jesus Christ," he rasped. "The auditions are in two weeks. Car, what am I going to do?"

"You're going to take this injury seriously, and you're going to stay off that damn foot. In a few days, we'll take a look at it, if it's not any better, you're going to the hospital."

The elevator dinged at the fourth floor. Sighing, Alex let go of the rail and immediately Carolynne sidled in beside him to take his weight. She held onto him, serving as a crutch as they made their way down the darkened hall to Alex's apartment. Thank God his parents didn't mind paying for it and didn't require him to have a job. He would be screwed right now otherwise.

After fishing his key from his pocket, he unlocked the door and it sprung wide open. Cool air hit his face, and only then did he realize how hot he actually was. The summer sun had been warm, very warm, but Alex suspected some of that heat came from his pain.

Carolynne immediately walked him over to the couch. She sat him down then went right to stacking pillows at one end. "Put it up here," she demanded, patting the fluffy pile.

He spun around and kicked his foot up as ordered after taking off his shoes. When the blood started to flow back up his leg and away from his foot, the throbbing in his head and injured appendage slowly subsided. He let out a sigh of relief as his eyes fluttered closed.

"Is there anything else I can get for you, sweetie?" Carolynne asked.

"No." Alex licked his lips. "Unless you want to send that beautiful brother of yours my way."

"Alexander Benton," she barked, stomping her foot at him. "I'm not doing it. You need to rest, not to screw all night."

"Carolynne"—Alex sat up, elbows supporting his torso— "why do you think I just want to have sex with your brother? Maybe I want to spend time with him. Maybe I don't want to be alone."

She gave him a droll stare.

"I'll behave, I swear. Just tell him to come keep me company. Besides, do you want to wait on me hand and foot? I know *he* will."

"Fine, but I'm going to be checking in on you guys, and you'd *better* be behaving."

Alex couldn't help laughing. That motherly thing she did to him always cracked him up. While he might have hated it with anyone else, he adored it in Carolynne. Her attention made him a little less homesick than he might've been otherwise.

The door closed behind her, snapping shut with a loud bang. Alex carefully rolled over on the couch, and as he reached for the remote, he looked down and got a clear sight of his foot. It wasn't red and swollen anymore, but had actually started turning purple. Alex freaked. Without his feet, he wouldn't have any kind of future in dance.

He wiggled his toes and the pain that tore through him blinded him momentarily. A heart-stopping scream ripped from his lips. His pained cries lingered even as his front door opened again and the sound of heavy feet stomped toward him. Kenneth appeared in his wavering vision.

Alex rasped, "Something's wrong."

"Do you want me to get Carolynne?" Kenneth asked.

"No." Alex grabbed Kenneth's hand, still panting and cringing from the pain. "Don't leave. Call her and tell her something is wrong."

With one hand around Alex's, Kenny used his free hand to dig in his jeans for his phone. Alex watched him fumble the device, trying not to drop it while dialing Carolynne. The longer it took for his best friend to answer, the more Alex wanted to break down and cry. Fear and pain and the heartache of watching his dreams slip away weighed on him hard, so hard he trembled.

Then he distantly heard Kenny speaking to Carolynne. He

heard Kenny tell her that Alex was freaking out and crying, that he'd said something wasn't right and she needed to come immediately. Apparently, the conversation ended because Kenny hung up the phone and set it down on the table beside them. He looked at Alex and said, "She's on her way."

Kenneth sat down on the floor, still holding Alex's hand tightly. As long as Alex didn't move, everything seemed to be okay, everything save for his dreams of dancing crumbling around his purple foot. He closed his eyes and laced his fingers with Kenny's, silently praying he hadn't managed to end his life by chasing after a part that would've never made or broken his career.

CHAPTER SEVEN

"Are you all right?"

Augusto looked up and blinked at the guy beside him. It was the smoker from earlier.

"I know that look." He grinned. "It's the look of '*I got in! Now what?*' Am I right?"

"Yeah. Did you get in too?"

The guy nodded. "Jason Nazuzaka," he said, extending a hand. "You are?"

"Augusto Catalan. They call me Gus." Augusto accepted Jason's hand and shook before releasing it. "It's like surfacing for air after a long swim underwater, you know?"

"Haven't heard it put quite like that before but you're right. I guess I'll be seeing you around and get to see what kind of trouble Alexander can cook up for you."

Augusto rolled his eyes. "Please. Not my fault he has a stick up his ass. I have to go. I want to tell my best friend the good news and figure out a way to pay for my tuition here."

Jason laughed. "Where do you work now?"

"I dance at Santo's."

"They'll frown on that," Jason told him. "Something about outside injuries and picking up bad habits. I guess they want to be the one to smash your dreams into a million pieces. If you're not going to tell them, don't get injured."

Augusto made a face as they began walking south on Broadway toward the Columbus Circle Station. He couldn't quit Santo's since he wasn't remotely good at anything else. And even if he asked for another job at the club, it'd break his heart not being able to dance on that stage. It had nothing to do with the fear of getting a new job—the trepidation came with the thoughts of leaving Santo's, not making it in Julliard and not being able to go back to Santo's. Only the best graduated and if he didn't make it, he wanted a way to still be able to grace a stage. The happiness he felt about his acceptance suddenly vanished and all he wanted to do was curl into a ball. Deep down, Augusto knew his fear was irrational. Luther would always let him go back to dance at Santo's but sweat still flowed down his brow.

He stopped at the station's entrance and thumbed over his shoulder. "This is where I stop."

"I'll see you around—are you a dance major?"

Augusto nodded. "Not much of an actor."

"I'll see you later."

Augusto watched Jason walk away and climb into a cab. He wasn't that crazy. Taking a cab in the city had *bad idea* written all over it because New York was one large traffic jam no matter the time of the day. A cab ride would cost way too much money. He found his transit pass and his music. After sticking the buds into his ears, he jogged down the steps listening to *LMFAO*.

But even the upbeat tempo couldn't cheer him up. When he walked through the door, Keith did an almost comical slide from the kitchen to face him.

"Gimme the news," Keith demanded with hope in his eyes. "Why do you look like someone died?"

"I got in."

"That's great! Wait…no?"

"It is great. I don't want to seem ungrateful. I just found out I may not be able to work at Santo's anymore."

"What do you mean you won't be working at Santo's anymore?"

"The school frowns on outside dancing," Augusto explained. He walked by Keith into the living room and pulled his bag over his neck. He dropped it to the sofa then plopped down beside it. Lifting his feet to the center table, he rested his head back, slipping down comfortably. "They don't want me getting injured or some bullshit like that. Where am I going to get another job?

I'm not good at anything else and I have to work!"

"I'm sorry, man." Keith sat beside him and pulled him into a hug.

Augusto couldn't remember the last time he felt so weak. He just had one success but had to give something up. It wasn't just anything. Dancing at Santo's meant the world to him. It made him happy. "Why do I have to give up my one bit of happiness so I can have another? Why do I have to choose? Why is it always like that?"

"I don't know, Gus. But maybe you should talk to the boss about getting back behind the counter."

"I couldn't stay there. Watching all those dancers and not being able to join them would do some damage. I'm not that strong." Augusto sat back from his friend's arms. "And being stuck only able to dance in class would kill me. Then I would be like all those other drones you see dancing because their joy has been sucked out of them. I didn't know I'd have to give up my freedom to be a part of this school."

"Your freedom? *Dramático mucho?*"

"I'm not being dramatic! Dancing is freedom for me."

"It's only for a little while, Gus. Come on, don't fall on me now."

Augusto wanted desperately to tell him he was already falling. But the truth was he had nothing else to lose. He was going to have to ask for his old job behind the bar and go back to dancing only for fun on the dance floor and not on the stage.

"This sucks," he muttered after a while.

Keith took his hand and squeeze affectionately. "Baby chunks. But you can do this."

"Thanks, Keith."

"I told you. I got your back."

CHAPTER EIGHT

Alex leaned the one crutch he agreed to use against his teacher's desk. He felt like an idiot hauling that thing around, an idiot because what experienced dancer breaks a toe practicing for an audition? Well, according to the emergency room doctors, he was one such idiot. Now, he was toting around a crutch and sporting a not-so-attractive walking boot, and to make matters worse, he'd been told no dancing for a month. Which meant his chances for playing the role of Franz in Coppelia were completely blown. Needless to say, his disposition had been on the gloomy side of sunny for a week now.

Monday morning meant the new dancers would be joining the freshman ballet class for the first time. If nothing else, those poor fools might keep him entertained…maybe. He sat down next to Madame Margot, his favorite of all his teachers, and slid a doctor's note across the desk to her.

"No dancing for a month. Then, I have to get clearance from the docs."

"That is *pas bon, mon élève*," she responded in her native French.

"No. It's no good at all."

"You will observe, *qui?*"

"*Qui*," he said flatly.

"The new students, they will be in class today. I fear they may need your assistance. You will help them, *non?*"

"As long as it doesn't include dancing, I'll do anything you need me to do, Madame."

"*Très bien.*"

Voices carried down the hallway. Students piled into the classroom. The experienced ones took their normal places, standing at the barres comprising individual rows. They worked to stretch out their muscles— relevé, en pointe, relevé, demi-pointe. Alex would've given anything to be warming up with them, even though they were just freshmen.

With a sigh, he looked back over at the door and caught the Latino boy from the audition broaching the entrance. A wicked grin graced Alex's lips. "Well, what do we have here?" he all but purred. "The boy from the barrio made it. Congratulations."

"I see the asshole didn't wash off you over the weekend," the new kid replied.

"Now, now, is that any way to speak to an upper classman?"

"Is that how you think it's going to work around here?"

Alex leaned up from his chair, both palms pressed to his teacher's desk. The edges of his lips curled. He said, "I suggest you find your place quick, freshman. There are standards around here. There are traditions, unwritten rules on how one should behave. I suggest you learn those rules. And, sweetie, don't get on my bad side or you'll never grace the stage. Understood?"

The new guy smiled and tilted his head. He stepped just a tad closer to the desk and leaned in. "Your bad side? If it looks anything like your face, there's nothing to be afraid of—just laugh at." He made to leave but stopped then faced Alex. "And by the way, don't call me sweetie. You're not my type."

He walked off again and only stopped to bump fists with a Japanese student.

Freshmen, so childish.

Alex sat back down at the desk, then reached for one of the lower drawers and opened it so he could prop his foot on its face. He couldn't be bothered with the new boy right now. He couldn't even bring himself to get angry. Maybe that had more to do with the fact he had a nice dose of painkillers in him and less to do with the fact the new kid wasn't completely unattractive.

"We start every class standing in the first position, *qui*," Margot said.

Everyone in the class stood with their feet flat, heels together, toes apart, arms bent slightly, hands at their waists. Everyone save for the new guy. He looked around the room and struggled to imitate his classmates. It took everything Alex had not to burst into laughter.

Margot continued to bark moves at them all. Most knew every move, from the simplest to the most complex. Then there was the new kid, who was completely lost. Honestly, Alex had a moment of sorrow for him. Alex had been in his shoes less than a year ago, but at least he had been in ballet since the age of six. He'd chosen different forms of dance over the varied sports the other boys chose to play—something the new kid should've done as well.

"Alexander," Margot called from across the room. She had her hand wrapped around the new kid's wrist. "Please, go to one of the free rooms and work with him. I can do nothing with him. He knows nothing."

"Yes, ma'am," Alex said as he stood from her desk. He grabbed his single crutch and tucked it under his arm, nodding toward the door. "Come on, freshman."

Instead of following right away, the new guy turned and said something to the Japanese guy who nodded. The two exchanged a few words before Latino guy brushed by Alex hard. The move almost knocked Alex right off his feet. He waited until they got out into hallway before tearing into the kid.

"Hey, you fucking mind?" He looked down at his broken foot. "I'm kinda having issues here."

"Kinda having issues?" He whirled on Alexander. "Man, I don't even know you and I want to punch you in the face!"

"Well, I wouldn't suggest that if you want to stay here. Now, do you want to learn these moves or not?" Alex thumbed over his shoulder. "Because I can tell Margot you'd rather beat my ass than do as she asked."

"You can tell her whatever you want. As for this—it's up to you. We can either have you teach me and you act like less of a dick or I can find someone else to help."

Alex hobbled closer. In a low voice, he said, "The best thing you can do for yourself is work with me. You *want* me to teach you because I'm the best this school has to offer right now. I've been in ballet since childhood. I know every possible move anyone can throw at you. I can make you perfect. Is that something you want, or would you rather be stubborn and flunk out? Now,"—Alex offered his hand— "I'm Alex. And you are?"

He said nothing for a moment. "Augusto."

"Okay, Augusto." Alex dropped his hand. "If you would follow me over to that room"—he nodded toward a door on the other side of the hall—"then we can get started."

CHAPTER NINE

Jason told him to behave himself and while Augusto didn't promise he would—he promised he would try. But Alexander Benton was testing his damn patience. As the dancer barked instructions at Augusto, he tried his very best to catch them.

Ballet?

What kind of mindless jerk forces a hip-hop dancer to do ballet? Do they not know cruel and unusual punishment is illegal?

Still, he tried learning what Alexander taught him. It wasn't easy getting the moves. His troubles were compounded by the fact he had an intense dislike for the ass teaching them to him.

First position.

Second position.

The whole thing sound like sexual positions. Being in the room with Alexander killed any carnal feelings he could have imagined in him. He stopped and straightened his back, relaxed his shoulders, bringing his arms before his body in the first position. He turned his feet but just couldn't get them as far as they needed to go. His body didn't bend that way.

"This is ridiculous," he muttered in frustration. "There is no way to get this."

"It's not easy," Alex admitted. "It takes practice. You need to stretch your muscles first. Limber up a bit."

"Limber up a bit?" Augusto frowned and walked away from Alexander to stare out the glass window for a brief moment. He raked his fingers through his damp hair and wondered when he'd started sweating so much. "Ballet isn't something I do."

From behind him, Augusto heard the metal legs of a chair raking against the floor. He glanced back long enough to see Alex sitting down, then turned his stare back to the window.

Alex said, "While I'm really trying to be understanding, I need you to understand that ballet is something you're going to have to do. If you want to dance in this school, it's not something you have a choice in. It's required." Alex paused long enough for Augusto to have a chance to light into his ass, but before he could turn around, aim and fire, Alex was speaking again. "I watched your routine at the auditions. You can do this, if you try. Your body can do these moves, but you have to want to do it first."

Augusto eyed him. "You think I don't want to do this? This is my last shot. This is it for me so I can't fuck it up. But that still doesn't change the fact that my body doesn't fucking bend the way ballet needs it to bend and even if I could somehow manage to do that—it'll never be good enough."

"Stop." Alex held up both hands. "You keep telling yourself that, you won't be good enough. Got it? Now, just…just try, okay? If you want, if you'll let me touch you, I'll help you."

The thought of Alexander touching him made him physically ill. It wasn't that Alexander wasn't a good-looking man—he was egotistic and mean, a whole different kind of ugly. Augusto pressed his back into the wall and folded his arms. He tilted his head to one side, took a breath and swallowed the lump in his throat. "I'll try it again," he told Alexander, easing away and straightening his body again.

"Very well." Alex sat back down. "Heels together. Toes apart. Relax your arms."

Augusto tried again.

It came around a little better. He straightened his knees as if he would be doing a front step in one of his routines. The move caused him to waver slightly on his feet and he had to stick his hands out to his sides in order to steady himself. He groaned and went for it again.

"You're doing fine," Alex encouraged. "Much better, this time. Try one more time, sweetie. Then we'll move on to second position."

Sweetie.

That word was beautiful once—when Kemar used it. Ignoring

it, he repeated the move until he could do the first position without wanting to fall over and the back of his knees didn't hurt. "Okay...first position."

"Perfect." Alex grinned, like genuinely smiled as if dancing made him happy enough to forget being an egotistical asshole. "Now, the second position is much easier. Put about six inches between your heels. Like this." Alex stood from his chair and positioned his legs like he wanted Augusto to do; even with a walking cast on one foot he managed just fine. "And hold your arms out like this." He lazily draped his arms out from his sides.

Augusto copied the move. It was a little rough on his knees and each time he wanted to quit, he thought of the guys who did that reality show on television. They had mere weeks to learn routines outside their genre and had to get it right or they got sent home. If they could do that, he could definitely do this. The second position came much easier—Alexander was right and soon he could go through the third and the fourth. The fifth position was another giant pain in the ass.

"Fuck," he groaned when he pulled his feet a little too far inward and toppled to the floor.

Alexander offered him a hand. There wasn't so much as a curl in his lips, not a condescending smile or anything like that. "Here. Let me help you up."

"You're going to help me up?" Augusto shuffled away. "You can barely stand."

"Hey, I'm doing okay...kinda." Alex half laughed. "I was only trying to be helpful. In a moment, when it's time to plié in between each position, you're going to *really* hate me."

I don't know who he's kidding—I hate him now.

He gave up on standing and simply looked up at Alexander. "Plié? What the hell is a plié?"

"I swear, if I fall on my face doing this, you keep that to yourself."

Alex licked his lips, closed his eyes and bent his knees. He went through each of the five positions almost fluidly, coming down on slightly bent knees before springing into the next position. When he landed in the fifth, he winced. His eyes shot open and he gasped down a deep breath.

"Are you all right?" Augusto shot to his feet to help him back to his chair. "We should stop for the day. I can keep practicing on my own and you should get some rest. I don't want to be blamed for any end of career injuries you may sustain."

Looking up, Alex quirked a brow. There wasn't anything egotistical or vain, nothing teasing in Alex's gaze. If Augusto didn't know better, he would swear he saw a little sadness.

"Be careful, sweetie," Alex said. "I might mistakenly think you care."

"Hold your breath," Augusto said softly in a voice filled with sarcasm.

"I'm fine," Alex breathed, but clearly he wasn't.

"You don't seem fine. Here, sit down a sec." Augusto found himself softening and it worried him. He slipped to his knees and examined the cast not sure what he was looking for.

"Augusto, get up. I'm fine. I…I promise."

Taking a breath, Augusto rose. "We should stop for today. My muscles are complaining anyway."

"Not yet," Alex said, lifting himself up from the chair. He held on to Augusto's arm and for some stupid reason, Augusto didn't bother pulling away. They were nose to nose, staring down at each other's lips. "Complaining muscles are a good thing. Besides, I have more to teach you," Alex whispered. "Much more."

Everything in Augusto told him to pull away. His brain reminded him he hated this guy. But something kept him there, watching the way Alexander's pink tongue flowed over his lips then disappeared into his mouth. His breath was hot against Augusto's face, sending a slight shiver down Augusto's spine. "Yeah, but I'll be late for my next class."

"Be late."

"First impressions, Alexander."

"I'll get you out of it."

"I can't," Augusto replied, but he tilted his head like he would to fit their lips perfectly together. "I should go. I'll see you tomorrow." But he didn't move.

"Just kiss me already," Alex said breathlessly, tilting his head in the opposite direction.

An audible intake of breath echoed through the room as Augusto smirked and eased in slightly. He ensured his breath played over Alexander's skin. His lips, a mere pucker away from his *teacher*. "That would make your day, Alexander. I guarantee it. But I ain't easy." Augusto took a step back then left the room, feeling as if he was walking on air. He wasn't sure what—but something had happened in that room, something he couldn't allow to happen ever again.

CHAPTER TEN

Exhaling sharply, Alex sank down onto the chair. He stretched his body out and let his head hang backward. His groin now ached for someone's touch or someone's mouth or…something. The throbbing had to stop. He had to fix this and fast. Alex reached down and gripped himself, moaning as a wave of instant relief rolled through him. But despite the comforting sensation, he knew the moment he let go, it would be all hands on deck again and his buddy downstairs would start banging around in his pants for a little more attention.

He didn't want to move from that spot, fearing an embarrassment of the worst possible kind—his wood pitching tent in his nylon gym pants. The aching and throbbing down below meant just the right touch would push him over the edge and while he could've rubbed one out right then, there was something almost desperate and demeaning about it, especially after being rejected by a guy like Augusto Catalan, and a freshman no less.

No, Alex had a reputation to uphold, and by God, if anyone walked in that room and caught him doing anything, it would be someone going down on him and not him relieving himself because a beautiful Latino boy had gotten under his damn skin.

"The nerve," he growled as he reached in his pocket and dug for his phone. Once he had the contraption in his hand, he sent a quick text to Kenny.

Get to room 212…NOW!

Kenneth would've been at the school anyway, getting ready to head to his junior music composition class—a class Kenneth didn't need because he knew how to compose music better than anyone Alex had ever met. And thankfully, his dear sweet Kenneth was the kind of man who liked making people happy; one of the good guys, he probably deserved so much better than Alex. For some stupid reason though, Kenneth came to Alex's every beck and call. He was like an eager puppy, bouncing around, waiting for someone to throw him a ball.

Jesus, where is he?

As Alex waited for Kenneth's arrival, he closed his eyes and massaged his groin, keeping the blood flowing, keeping himself hard. He couldn't help imagining Augusto's hand attentively tending to his erection—gently stroking, rousing his release. A groan wound up his body and pushed through his parted lips. He could already feel that beautiful Latino boy's mouth on his, even after he heard Kenneth say, "I'm here. Are you okay?"

"Kneel down," Alex said, pointing between his slightly spread legs. "I need a blowjob."

"You *need* a blowjob?"

"Desperately."

"Why?"

"Will you please stop asking stupid questions and get on your damn knees?" Alex sighed, realizing what an asshole he sounded like. "Please?" he said with a little more kindness.

Kenneth hesitated. For the first time since they'd started these ongoing trysts, he saw a look of defiance pass over his part-time lover's handsome features. Lips pursed, brows furrowed, Kenneth stared at Alex. But as soon as he saw Alex massaging his own groin, something in Kenny's expression changed.

Eyeing him hard, Alex watched Kenneth lock the door then drop his backpack next to the only barre in the very center of the room. Alex hooked his thumbs on the waist of his nylon pants then pulled them down far enough for his rock hard cock to spring free. It jutted out from his thighs, thick and perfectly ready to feel Kenneth's lips riding over his skin.

The moment he felt Kenneth's mouth sheathing his cock, Alex closed his eyes and relaxed in the seat. Kenneth whipped his talented tongue over and under Alex's shaft, licked around the head and rode back down again. It was perfect, absolutely wonderful, but Alex realized the perfection of the moment came from him imaging Augusto kneeling down between his thighs and lovingly embracing his cock with his warm, spicy mouth, not the talents of Kenneth's tongue or the fact he'd come running the moment Alex texted him.

Suddenly, Alex felt like one of those men he abhorred so much—those men who never wanted to get to know someone, who only wanted a quick fuck and nothing meaningful. All the men his age pretty much fit into that spectrum. They were one of two reasons Alex had become so cold in the first place, and now he was placing that frigid chill in his heart on poor Kenneth.

"What's wrong?" Kenneth asked, right after Alex's cock slipped from his mouth.

"Nothing. Why?" Alex lied.

"You're not being as…I don't know…forceful as you normally are."

"Sorry. I guess I got distracted." Alex brushed his hand over Kenny's hair. "Continue. Please."

Kenneth's head dipped back down and the moment his warm mouth embraced Alex's cock, Alex thought he would come unglued. The short conversation hadn't taken away from the sensitivity, surprisingly. In fact, the warm rush after the cool breeze seemed to make things more intense than they had been. And despite feeling like shit for using Kenny, he still couldn't get Augusto out of his mind.

He reached down and knotted his fingers in Kenny's hair, picturing Augusto's thick black locks twining around his digits. It wasn't that he intentionally forgot about Kenny or didn't enjoy Kenny. He did very much, in fact, but right now, the way Augusto had rejected him, Alex simply couldn't help himself.

"I'm about to come," Alex rasped, giving Kenneth his due warning.

Kenny pumped again and again. A few deep thrusts and Alex was nearly jack-hammering himself off the chair. Heat rushed to the head of his cock and exploded in Kenny's mouth. Kenny didn't stop sucking and licking and thrusting his mouth down over Alex's length. Alex could barely do more than pant. He loosened his fingers in Kenny's hair and let his arm fall to his sides.

"You okay?" Kenneth asked, wiping at his lips.

"I'm fine," Alex rasped. "You mind helping me get home?"

"Not at all."

Before helping Alex up from the chair, Kenneth grabbed his backpack and situated it on his shoulders. Then he hooked his arm under Alex's. Alex snuggled into his side, taking his crutch with him. He laid his head on Kenneth's shoulder and suddenly felt incredibly guilty about what had just happened.

"Do you love me?" he asked softly, without looking at Kenny, silently praying for Kenny to say no.

"Never really thought about it," Kenny said after a moment of quiet. "I mean, Carolynne told me not to get wrapped up in you. She said you weren't the settling down type. Why? You love me?"

God, why did I bring this up?

He lifted his head and looked up at Kenny. His beautiful lover kept his head forward, paying close attention to where he walked and how he held Alex. Kenny was careful enough to make sure nothing he did hurt Alex. Seeing Kenny in that light made Alex's guilt even worse.

No, he didn't love Kenny. No, he didn't want to settle down with Kenny. He loved having sex with Kenny, loved the way Kenny did everything he was asked and how he took care of everything Alex wanted. He loved the idea of Kenny and how he could rely on his lover for anything and everything. But no, he didn't love Kenny at all.

"Alex, you okay?" Kenny asked.

"I'm...I'll be fine," Alex spoke quietly.

CHAPTER ELEVEN

"I hear you got into Julliard." Chet sat beside Augusto.

Someone has a big mouth.

Chet would find out sooner or later but he wanted to be the one to tell him. Augusto groaned as he stretched his legs out. He'd spent the whole week doing pliés and squats and first positions, second positions—leaving his whole body one big ache. Then add in rehearsals for Santo's and it was getting to be too much. Every time he looked at Luther and opened his mouth to ask for a new position, Augusto's heart wouldn't allow it; especially so soon before their BDSM theme night.

Rubbing a hand against his aching neck, he lifted his feet to the small table in the middle of the room. "Yeah. Been there a week and already want to slit my wrists."

"It can't be that bad. I'd rather be there than here."

"I'm sure. Why don't you try again?"

"I'm almost thirty, Gus. No one wants a washed up, thirty year old joining their prestigious school."

"Who told you that?"

Chet tied his laces and stood. "It's reality. You're still young. You have something special and they saw it. Me? I have the same *good* as every other dancer out there. I ain't swag or any of that shit."

"Can you hear the bullshit coming out of your mouth?" Augusto stood to go toe-to-toe with Chet. "Who says crap like that? It's not easy—of course not. It sucks most times. I have some upperclassman who hates my ass just for breathing and a bunch of teachers who think I'm a machine. Then the wealthy kids who treat me like a leper—and that's all of them! It's not easy but you at least have to try. What is it that you think I have that you don't?"

"*It.* You have what they call *it.* Look at you. You're good-looking, big brown eyes, thick, amazing hair and those pouty lips that could make a straight man cry. You have the body of a sculpted Adonis but most importantly, you have this heart inside your chest most of us wish we had. You want to know what I learned over the years of auditioning and having doors slam in my face?"

"What's that?"

"Not everyone who loves to dance should."

"Chet…"

His friend merely exited the room, closing the door silently behind him. Augusto took a breath and rested his hands on his hips. After a moment of waiting to see if Chet would come back, he tried focusing on the night's performance. But someone knocked on the door, interrupting his peace. He thought it was the other dancers beginning to come in but Keith stuck his head in.

"Hey, roomie. Was beginning to think I lived alone lately."

"You made it!" Augusto laughed. "I'm sorry I keep missing our work-outs in the morning. But lately I've been so tired." He hugged Keith tightly, needing to feel his strength. When he stepped back, Keith lifted Augusto's chin and their gazes locked.

"It's all right. I understand. Why do you look so uncertain?"

"Remember that guy I told you hated my guts?"

"Asshat with the attitude?" Keith asked then sat in Augusto's chair. He reached for one for Augusto's apples on the dresser and bit into it. "Talk to me."

"Well, they're forcing me to learn ballet; at least the basics. Apparently they have it in their heads that I need to be a well-rounded dancer to pass the program. So, now they have him tutoring me."

"He's the best, right?"

"Yes and he won't let me forget it. But something happened—we got kind of close and I wanted to kiss him."

Keith bit the apple, his teeth crunching through the fruit echoed in the room. "But you don't like him."

"I don't. But it doesn't matter if I like him. Liking him or not liking him has nothing to do with a good, rough fuck. I mean he has a crutch and I'm seriously thinking of using it to hold him down and…"

"Hrm."

Augusto sat on the center table facing Keith. "I hate it when you do that. What's *hrm*? Is that even a word?"

"I'm thinking. Would you stop being *douchie* for a second? Look, if you don't like this guy you can't just have sex with him. You're better than that. Don't be one of those men who go around just sticking their cocks into every hole they find. Sooner or later it'll fall off."

"Is this one of those things like if you masturbate too much you'll go blind?"

Keith laughed. "I'm being serious here! Just be careful around this guy. I've never met him and I want to punch him in the face."

Augusto remembered his conversation with Alexander and laughed too. "Yeah—that seems to be the general consensus."

"Why are you thinking so hard about this?" Keith questioned. "It's not like you want him."

"I know. We have nothing in common. He's mean just to be mean and seems to be all out for himself. He's the exact opposite of every man I've ever dated and he's against everything I believe in."

Someone else knocked on the door and one of the stage guys stuck his head in. "Start heading for the stage, Gus. Oh by the way, a Jason's here?"

"Thanks, Ben. I'm coming."

Ben nodded and closed the door again.

"Jason?" Keith questioned with a wiggle of his brows.

"It's not like that. Jason is one of the guys I met at school. He's a good kid—great dancer. And he's a looker. If you're interested I could hook you up."

"Oh no." Keith waved his hand. "I swore I'd stay single until I graduate. Besides, the men you find are not my type."

"Your loss." Augusto reached in and bit the apple still in Keith's hand, kissed his cheek and headed for the door. "Come on. Enjoy the show."

"Before you go, when was the last time you heard from Donny?"

Augusto's heart stopped for a moment, then hammered furiously in his chest. "Two weeks. I'm trying not to think about it."

"No news is good news."

"The idiot who came up with that should be found and shot. I have to go."

"Break a leg!"

August grinned and let himself out. As he made his way toward the stage he thought about Alexander and wondered if that moment they had was just one of those times because they so disliked each other. Frowning, he pushed his way through the first row of curtains, upset with himself. There was no way Alexander the Great was thinking about him. Augusto was beneath him—wasn't that the gist of what Alexander had said when he first got there? Disgusted with himself, he waited until Ben came out again and they walked in to sit in the meeting circle with the other dancers.

"Didn't think you were joining us," Ben teased.

Augusto smiled and sat beside Chet.

CHAPTER TWELVE

The next morning, Alex waited in the private room where he'd taught Augusto the day before, the very same room where Kenneth had serviced him after the beautiful Latino boy had inadvertently roused a very significant problem in Alex's loins. He leaned against a window that overlooked the traffic zooming past Lincoln Center.

The early morning sky bleeding in behind him was awash in hues of pink, gold and purple. Alex put his weight on his good foot, arms crossed over his chest, burning a hole through the door with his stare. As far as he was concerned, Augusto owed him for that mess yesterday, owed him big for making him feel like a lousy human being and an even more pathetic man. Augusto didn't know it, but he'd stolen something simple and pure from Alex, and that was his salacious little trysts with a man he cared about but didn't love.

When the door creaked, Alex's eyes found a focus they hadn't had before. He'd been staring, but not really looking. Now, he concentrated on the opening in the doorway, and what he found was Augusto at the end of his very pointed stare.

"I think we should talk," Alex said, keeping his voice nice and calm. "You really messed me up yesterday."

Augusto dumped his bag in a corner and began to peel his outer shirt from his body. "Messed you up? I don't remember doing anything to you. What are you on about?"

"You rejected me," Alex replied flatly, watching as a very tight tank top hugging Augusto's very firm chest slowly became exposed. His mouth started to water. "People don't reject me. Why did you do that? Help me understand this."

The black shirt slid from Augusto's arms exposing toned, caramel shoulders. "I rejected you?" He shook his head. "Alexander, start making sense. I'm not in the mood for riddles today."

"Yesterday, in this very room," Alex said, closing the distance between them. "I told you to kiss me. You were so close, so ready. I wanted you to just kiss me and you told me you weren't easy right before bolting straight out of this room." He searched Augusto's face. "Why did you do that?"

"I didn't bolt anywhere." Augusto frowned. "And I didn't kiss you because it wouldn't have done either of us any good."

"Why? How can you say that when you don't know?"

"I'm tired, Alexander. So let's cut to the chase. I don't do drama. I don't do ego and I don't do stuck up. You are all these things wrapped into one big ball of confusion and I'm so confused. So can we just practice so I can go?"

With a frown of his own, Alex took a few steps back. He ground his teeth, inhaling so sharply it flared his nostrils. Those were all signs of true hurt, hurt he sure as hell didn't want Augusto to see because he didn't deserve to have that part of Alex. Not yet. Probably not ever. "Fine," Alex said bitterly. "You're such hot shit. Dance for me."

Augusto backed up before turning away from Alex. There was something heady in the way the Latino hottie looked at Alex, something knowing and daring and antagonistic, as if he knew exactly how he affected Alex and would play off that knowledge until he made Alex crazy.

It was working…so far.

Augusto walked to the system in the corner and dragged his fingers along the music there. Alex watched Augusto's simple action with a strange appreciation. At one point he had to remind himself of the emotions surging through him. Finally, the sounds of a song began playing and Alex's curiosity flared with new zeal.

At first Augusto began in what Alex came to know as *his* style—a slow hip-hop type movement that was different than anything Alex had ever seen before. It was sexy and exotic, and Augusto's body moved like soft silk in time with the music. He then slipped quite seamlessly into the five different positions he'd learned the first day, arms and legs moving fluidly, like ribbons wisping through the air. Each move of his head caused his hair to flow with the action. Alex couldn't deny wanting to feel those thick locks wrapped around his fist.

There had to be a reason Augusto chose that song. Even as he'd used the whole space, dancing around Alexander, he'd made no physical contact but there was a stark emotion in his eyes.

The last line of the chorus was sung—*Love never looked so good on you*—and Alex would've sworn he'd begun to melt right where he stood.

By the time the song drew to an end, Augusto stood on the far side of the room with his back pressed to the wall, his face turned so he was looking over his right shoulder. His chest heaved with exertion.

Alex could barely breathe. That wonderfully lewd look in Augusto's eyes made something odd and dangerous and absolutely exhilarating come to life in Alex. He realized then that this man, this very sexual, very talented, and completely mysterious man was someone he had to have. And Alex would make a fool of himself trying…maybe.

"Come here," he said quite tensely, not giving away any of the emotion he now felt. No, the words were commanding and as forward as they came.

"What? Didn't I do it right?"

"Ironically, you did the ballet moves perfectly. In fact, even the ones I'm sure you weren't aware of were executed well. But that's not what I want." Alex held out his pointer finger, crooked and signaled for Augusto to do as he'd asked. "Come here."

Augusto eased from the wall, his head tilted slightly to the left, feet slowly dragging. The anticipation was enough to drive Alex insane. Despite his wanting to run across the room and rip Augusto up off his feet, Alex didn't move. He wouldn't do it. He wouldn't meet this gorgeous man halfway. What he wanted from Augusto, he demanded, and if the hunky dancer didn't give in this time, well, his loss.

The man stopped mere inches from Alex, his chest brushing

Alex's each time he breathed. Augusto reached up, wrapped his surprisingly long fingers against the back of Alex's neck and pulled him forward. Their breaths mingled before Augusto slammed his mouth over Alex's in a form of storming.

It stole the very last breath Alex had dared to breathe, seized his heart and rattled him to the very core of his being. While he'd wanted that kiss so badly, fantasized about it to the point of arousing himself, he never once expected it to happen, and even as Augusto's tongue dove deep into the dark corners of his mouth, Alex wondered if this was real or just some brutal fantasy.

CHAPTER THIRTEEN

The kiss left him feeling wild. Something within him snapped and it scared him. He never had that crazy, almost obsessed greed for a man's mouth before and it had to end. Donny explained it to him once—one day he would find someone to make him completely primal and he prayed it wasn't Alexander. Alexander represented the money, fame and power sort. The dancer was the exact opposite of the kind of man Augusto wanted in his life—he wanted a husband. The kind of man he prayed for was one who would put him first and love him just as fiercely as Augusto would love him. Kemar had been that kind of man but the universe was holding a grudge against something Augusto had done in a previous life or made a mistake for and now Kemar was gone. Besides, Augusto didn't think one could find that love twice in a lifetime.

Alexander couldn't be that man.

He tried a few times to pull back—to stop the madness, but Alexander's tongue would touch his, leaving him trembling and pressing forward into Alexander's chest. First, he released Alexander's neck, then pulled his arousal back from the dancer. It wasn't supposed to have happened. Augusto ripped his mouth away and instantly his head went down. He backed up slowly.

"That cannot happen again," he whispered. For a brief moment, he wasn't quite sure what to do with himself.

He merely wanted to give Alexander what he wanted so he would get over it already. But it backfired. The last thing he wanted to do was to show Alexander any other emotions so he quickly lifted his head and raked his hair back. In that moment, he pulled himself together before he turned his gaze back to Alexander. They couldn't kid themselves. That kiss was just something they had to get out of their systems and with it out, they could move on.

Right?

"We both know this cannot happen again," Augusto stressed.

Alexander opened his kiss swollen mouth to speak and apparently words failed him because he slammed his mouth shut again. He sat down on the window ledge, gripping the lip so hard his knuckles turned white. Augusto caught sight of a not so slight bulge between Alex's thighs.

"I don't know what to say. I…I didn't expect you to do that," Alex said breathlessly.

Augusto smiled and gathered his things. Before walking out the door, he glanced over his shoulder at Alexander. "It's fine. When was the last time you got what you wanted and it left you not knowing what to say?"

"Don't leave," Alex called, lifting himself back to his feet. He winced. "Please, don't leave again."

"Come on, Alexander. Who are we kidding? What are we really doing here? We both know you hate my guts and I can't say I particularly like you either."

"Who said I hated you? Jesus Christ, could you be anymore off the mark? If I hated you, do you honestly think I would be here right now? I'm not supposed to be dancing, ergo, not in class. I could've stayed home today, but I didn't. I didn't because I *wanted* to see you."

"No. You're here because a teacher told you to be here. And as big a jerk as you've been to me since my audition you don't seem to have the nerve to say no to her." Augusto strung his bag over his shoulder. "I'm not sure what your issue is with me but I'm not playing this game with you."

Clenching his jaw so tight the skin rippled over his jawbone, Alexander turned his head, casting his stare down toward the floor. In a hushed voice he said, "Fine. Then why are you still here?"

It dawned on Augusto then he wasn't quite sure why he'd stuck around. Though Alexander asked him not to go, Augusto couldn't put his finger on why he'd even entertained the idea that Alexander might ask for something else.

By the time he walked into his Lyrical Jazz class, he felt as if his body had been through the wringer. He was severely exhausted both physically and emotionally. He was also relieved he was the first in class so he could pull it together, but his alone time didn't last long because soon Jason walked in and flopped beside him.

"I feel like dirt," Jason muttered. "What's up with you?"

"Nothing. Stupid shit."

"I see. Are you ready for this class? Ms. Patterson is drilling us hard and not in a good way."

Augusto had to laugh then. "Never heard it put that way before. Hey, listen, I'm doing this major show down at Santo's on Saturday. I was given a few VIP tickets and I can give them to whoever I want." He hurried over to his backpack and pulled out the two passes. "I saved you one and then I have one extra one if you have a friend you want to invite."

Jason accepted them. "I don't have many of those. I'm sorta new in the country."

"Well if you meet someone you want to take then you have the extra one."

Jason nodded and went to stash them away in his bag. "I know we haven't known each other that long." He sat beside Augusto again. "But I know when something is bothering you. Besides, you look like you were kissed really well recently. Either that or you got bitten by a spider on the lip or something."

Augusto's hands instantly went up to touch his lips. He could feel they were slightly swollen and he was ashamed of what he'd done. Alexander hadn't asked to be kissed.

"Yeah, I kissed someone."

"Here? Did you meet someone?"

"Jason—I'm gay. You know that, right?"

"Yes. I knew that. I saw the way you were watching Mr. Wellington. I swore you were going to jump him."

"And?"

Jason arched a brow. "And what?"

"What do you think about it?"

"It's fine." Jason shrugged. "I like my men myself. I don't know why people make such a big deal about someone being gay. My father flipped a lid and left my mother and me when he found out. I've been careful not to talk to many people about it since then. So—you met a man. Is it Wellington?"

"No it's not Wellington!" Augusto was incredulous.

"We'll finish this conversation later." Jason grinned as other students began to enter.

It had been mere weeks and already the new students were elitists. Augusto made up his mind again to not let it bother him. There was a bigger picture—a bigger goal than getting into drama with a bunch of people who didn't understand working for anything. He patted Jason on the shoulder and they took their place in the center of the room with the other students while they waited for the teacher. While they stewed and talked about frivolous things, Augusto couldn't help thinking of the kiss he'd shared with Alexander.

The straight up truth was he wanted Alexander. Just having his tongue shoved so far into Alexander's mouth, twisting over his made him want to growl. Alexander had been aroused. Augusto had felt his hardened cock shoving into his and that did something inside Augusto.

"Mr. Catalan?"

He looked up to see all the other students were standing and he was still on the floor. He quickly scrambled to his feet like an idiot.

"Are you with us today? We'll be doing routines from *Cabaret*."

"Yes ma'am." Augusto blushed. "I'm here."

CHAPTER FOURTEEN

By Saturday morning, the walking cast on Alex's foot was driving him insane. If he didn't fear for his career, he might've ripped the damn thing off and tossed it in a corner, never to be touched again. He lay back on the couch with his foot propped up on the arm. The blood from his leg rushed down into his chest and his toes started to tingle, but he did the best he could to ignore it. Unfortunately, when he stopped thinking about his busted foot, he started thinking about Augusto.

"Goddammit!" he growled, tossing the pillow that had been behind his head across the room.

"Easy, Tiger," Carolynne said, closing the front door behind her. She picked up the pillow on her way in then pitched it onto the chair where she normally sat when she came to visit. "What has your panties in a twist?"

"This cast is driving me insane."

"So take it off."

"What about my foot?"

"Have you tried moving your toes? Do they still hurt?"

"No. I don't know."

"Forget the cast for a minute. I was out shopping with Kenneth and I saw something I think you might be interested in."

Alex knew better. There was absolutely nothing in this world he would be interested in right now because his "interest" had been left with a sexy Latino dancer who would rather die than be in the same room with him.

Damn Augusto.

He ran his fingertips over his lips, still feeling the tingle of that unexpected kiss, and here it was five days later and he hadn't gotten over it yet. The intoxicating kiss still lingered so that every time he thought about Augusto pressed against him, tongue shoved in his mouth, his cock started to twitch with anticipation.

Down boy.

Pinching his legs together, Alex rolled over on the couch, hoping like hell Carolynne didn't notice the side effects of the kiss that had completely rocked his world. He noticed she had a piece of paper folded in her hand.

"What's that?"

"The thing you'll be interested in."

Alex rolled his eyes.

"Don't give me that look. You love me and this will be the most entertaining night of your life."

"So what is it?"

"BDSM night at Santo's."

"And I care because…?"

She unfolded the paper and held it right in front of Alex's face. Despite the crinkle in the page, he saw exactly what she'd seen when she grabbed it. Augusto, dead center, dressed in a leather harness and a black Speedo. His short black wisps of hair framed his handsome face, and he knew those eyes better than he knew anyone else's. Those eyes had burned straight through to his soul just before Augusto planted those absolutely heavenly lips against his.

"Forget it," Alex grumbled as he settled back on the couch. He draped one arm over his face to hide whatever expression he might be wearing. He didn't need Miss Nancy Drew Wannabe over there asking him why seeing a picture of someone he supposedly despised would make him blush, get turned on, get angry or otherwise.

"Why?" she asked, voice whiny as if he'd just stolen her lollipop or something.

"I don't feel like it."

"Why not?"

"I'm in a damn cast, or haven't you noticed?"

"Jesus, Alex. Your moods these days are really starting to suck, you know? What the hell is happening to you? Are you and Kenny fighting?"

"No," Alex snapped.

"Then what's wrong with you?"

"Nothing. I'm fine."

"So go with me tonight. It'll be fun. We can hang out like we used to and you can laugh while that uppity little prick makes a fool of himself on stage."

An angry growl rumbled in Alex's chest and the moment he realized he was making the sound he fought to reel it back in. He didn't like her talking about Augusto like that one bit, but if he let on about it bothering him so badly, that would lead to a whole bunch of questions he couldn't answer, especially since he was sort of, kind of, in a weird way seeing her brother.

"Fine. I'll go."

He sat up on the couch and tossed his legs over the edge before scrubbing his hands over his face. Truth be told, while part of him wanted to lie on that couch and dream his Saturday away, the other part of him looked forward to watching Augusto dance again, and in such a sexual way. The idea of seeing that dancer bound in leather and flowing about the stage made Alex's mouth water.

"I need to take a bath and get ready."

"That's fine. I can come back later. The show doesn't start until nine anyway."

"Is Kenneth going too?"

"No," she said, rolling her eyes again. "He has some stupid indie music thing he's doing. You know, one of those shows where everyone stinks and they wear too much patchouli to cover their BO?"

Alex couldn't help laughing. Despite Carolynne adoring her

brother, that was one thing she'd never been able to get into. She constantly made jokes about his type of crowd and often said if he would clean up a bit, ditch the hippies and find a little fashion, Alex might let him hang out with them.

Truthfully, tonight, Alex was more than happy Kenneth wouldn't be joining them. At least Carolynne would be too into the show to pay him any attention. So if the sight of Augusto spanking some boy's ass on stage made Alex get a little too hard, Carolynne would be none the wiser. Hopefully.

"I'll be back later tonight," she said as she stood from the chair. She laid a single soft kiss on his forehead, not so casually dropping the flyer onto the table right in front of him.

After she left, long after the door had closed and Alex heard the locks click into place, he grabbed the paper from the table and ran his finger over Augusto's image. Immediately, the feel of the rough page against his skin took him back to that morning in the private practice space, the way Augusto had moved around the room and the devilishly devious look he'd had in his eyes, as if the dance was the sex he would never have with Alex, a tease, a vicious tease meant to drive Alex insane with desire. Oh, it'd worked. In spades. Alex desired that man more than it was safe to admit. In fact, the thought of Augusto and the kiss had him reaching down to grip his groin.

He moaned at the sudden pressure, legs spreading wide, head rolling back against the couch. At first, his gripping and massaging started out innocently, or so he told himself. Before long, he was so hard and the image of Augusto was so real, Alex couldn't keep fighting the inevitable. He reached inside his sweats and released his begging erection. He wrapped his fingers around his shaft and started to stroke. Eyes closed, he licked his lips and went right back to that day with *his* dancer.

Fuck. Yes. All his.

CHAPTER FIFTEEN

It was too early to be awake. But at six in the morning, Augusto managed to get showered, get some clothes on and shave the hair off his face. When he entered the kitchen, Keith met him and handed over a cup of steaming coffee. Augusto moaned.

"You are a king amongst men."

Keith laughed softly. "You need all the energy you can get right now. You ready for tonight?"

"As ready as I'll ever be. I wanted to talk to you about something."

"Sounds serious."

Augusto took a deep breath, sipped from his cup then locked eyes with Keith. "I kissed Alexander."

"Whoa! Wait a minute. You can't just throw that thing at me!"

"Sorry. There was no easy way to lead into it."

Keith's shoulders rose and fell. "Are we talking about the same Alexander who you hate and who doesn't mince words about how he feels about you?"

Augusto took another sip from his coffee and rubbed the back of his neck with his other hand. When it was said out loud it suddenly sounded like a swear word or blasphemy. "I know. He's not even my type. I don't know what happened. It's just ...ugh, I'm so upset with myself."

"It happens. Life does. So you kissed a man. You're not the first person to get turned on by that kind of high-school-ish hate. Don't beat yourself up about it."

Augusto hugged Keith. "You coming tonight?"

"What kind of question is that? Of course I'm coming! And there are a couple of guys I'm bringing with me. They want to see your ass on stage."

"Right…" Augusto laughed and after one final sip he handed the cup back to his friend. He snagged his bag from where it was sitting already packed on the sofa, stopped to turn down the AC because Keith never remembered to do it before leaving and ducked out the door. "See you later!" he hollered.

Outside was still hotter than hell but he didn't want to get caught in the subway. Instead of heading underground, he walked toward Santo's. Even with the temperature, he shoved his hands into his pockets after sticking his earbuds in and hurried by a Jamaican restaurant on the corner. He stopped and waved at a few women who always had kind words for him. Continuing down the street, he took a shortcut beneath a construction bridge and emerged before a couple of stores on a side street.

A man waved at him, Augusto stopped and pulled the earbud from his ear. "Hey, Martin! Am I seeing you tonight?"

Martin gave him the thumbs up. "Of course. Seeing you naked will make my day."

"I'm not going to be naked!" Augusto replied, his cheeks heating up. The idea of being naked for Martin gave him so many beautiful ideas. Then again being naked for Alexander gave him those same damn ideas. He frowned and gave Martin a mock salute, stuck his buds back in and hurried along, stopping only to pick up a fruit salad and a bagel with cream cheese.

At Santo's, the place was all but deserted. He left his bag in his chair, changed into rehearsal gear and ate only the salad. Thoughts of Alexander took away his appetite so he gave up on the bagel and climbed the stairs.

Sitting at the piano in the empty rehearsal room brought back the one memory Augusto didn't want to think about. He slipped onto the seat behind the piano, found the key he wanted and tapped it in tune to a reggae love song. But his heart simply broke each time he heard those keys.

Augusto stared like a starving man at the keys. He missed Donny.

Before Donny was deployed, Augusto had been angry. He'd said some things he didn't mean and the night before Donny left it'd hit him just what a jerk he was as he walked into Santo's before all the other dancers and workers. Someone played from the piano in the main rehearsal space and the music swept through the building beautifully. He dropped his bag in his chair and rushed up the stairs to see who was playing. Then he heard the song Donny sang and all he could do was stand by the door, lean his head against the frame and listen with tears streaming down his face. Donny sat at the piano, his large frame that normally stood so proudly, was slumped slightly as Chris Brown's Don't Judge Me seeped from his lips.

He wanted to reach forward and hug Donny tightly, but Augusto couldn't move. While the song was going he just couldn't seem to make his brain communicate with the rest of his body. At the end of the song, Donny pulled his hands back from the keys and Augusto cleared his throat. Donny swung around, almost toppling the seat with his sudden shift of weight.

"Sorry. Didn't mean to startle you." Augusto wrapped his arms around himself. "I am you know."

"You're what?"

"Sorry. I'm sorry. I didn't mean for it to seem as if I was judging you or—" Augusto stopped. The words were all jumbled together in his head. If he hadn't paused, he would've said something hurtful again and the pain in Donny's eyes broke him in ways he never thought possible. "Donny, when I said I hated you. I didn't mean it."

"I know."

"I know you're disappointed in me for my outburst . I should have handled it better. Of course I know you didn't choose to leave but it's so hard to imagine not waking up and being able to call you if I need anything." Taking a few more steps into the room, Augusto allowed his arms to fall to his sides. They didn't stay there, however, because soon his words got tangled against his tongue and he shoved his fingers through his hair.

"I know this isn't what you would choose for me. But you're good at this dancing and this music thing. Mammie's good at everything. I'm good at the physical stuff."

"I don't want to lose you. You hear of men and women going on active duty and never coming back—or they come back…"

"Dead."

Augusto winced and jerked away from the pain of the word. But even when he walked over to the bar and leaned his back to it, that one word still scraped against his heart like jagged glass.

"Say it, Gus."

"I can't."

"Say it—dead."

"Don't make me."

Donny rose and walked to him, his large frame towering like a giant over him. Augusto swallowed the lump in his throat and boxed away the tear that toppled down his cheek. He trembled and pressed into Donny's chest when the larger man pulled him forward.

"I don't want you to die, Don. You're the only brother I'll ever have and I really…I don't want you to die."

Donny's arms went around him, pulling him into one of his infamous hugs that could cure all the aches in the world. But as Augusto stood in his brother's arms, feeling the hurt pulse through him, for the first time, Donny's hugs couldn't cure him.

"You're early!" Luther called.

Augusto turned around to look at the man who would have been his father-in-law had his son not died. He rose and hugged him and watched Luther sit on the bench he'd vacated. "You all right? You seem tired."

"I've been better," Augusto replied. The last thing he wanted was to worry Luther with his thoughts of his brother. "Can I talk to you about something?"

"Of course."

"How would you feel if I started seeing someone?"

Luther leaned against the piano and fixed his stare on Augusto. His expression was unreadable and that scared Augusto deeply.

"Why would you ask me that?"

"Kemar was your son. Some fathers wouldn't want to see their son's lover seeing someone else after his death. You know I loved him more than I thought was possible…"

"Of course I know you loved him," Luther interrupted. "So do I. But he's dead, Gus. He's been dead for years. Loyalty is a beautiful thing but I don't expect you to stay alone for the rest of your life. You're young."

"You really mean that?"

Luther nodded. "But anyone you are with has to pass my test. You're a good kid, Gus. I don't want anyone to treat you any less than Kemar would have. He loved you, you know? I remember when he told me he was gay. He'd known for years but didn't tell me because he wasn't sure how I would take it. Then you two started dating and all of a sudden he found the courage to come right out and say, *'Dad I'm gay'.* I asked him why he was telling me—and if I didn't know what kind of man my son was before, I sure found out that day. He said he didn't want you to be a secret, said he loved you too much and you deserved to be claimed."

Sadness filled Luther's voice and eyes then. "Yeah, he was happy to be with you. The smile on my son's face was permanently plastered there. If he was alive you two would still be with each other. I know it. But it didn't work out like that. You know, me opening this place made it harder for him to come out of the closet. He thought I would think he was only saying he was gay because of this place. Anyways, I digress—he really was happy with you."

"He made me feel over the moon too. Smiling never came easy to me. But with Kemar, I found myself laughing sometimes until my sides hurt, tears would be streaming down my face and I wouldn't even know it. Those are the moments I remember the most—the small things like him picking me up Pralines and Cream ice cream on his way home. He hated the stuff but bought it because he knew I'm addicted to it. Or, I'd come to work and stick my hand into my pocket and there'd be a note from him. But you're right. As much as we love him, he's gone."

"Precisely. And Kemar wouldn't have wanted you to put your life on permanent hold. He would want to see you happy again."

"Is this one of those *if life gives you lemons* deals?"

Luther laughed and stood. "Don't worry so much. You have fun tonight. I know Juilliard isn't easy on their dancers. Use this as your breather."

Augusto hugged Luther again, held on to him and stole a little of his strength. "Thank you, for being here for me. I don't know if I've ever told you how much I appreciate everything."

"You don't have to say it, Gus. You've brought so much pleasure into my life. Please believe me when I say that."

"Thank you."

"Break a leg tonight." Luther chuckled.

Luther closed the door behind him and left Augusto alone in the rehearsal room again. He turned to look at the piano.

"Stay safe, Donny. Please stay safe."

Chapter Sixteen

Despite believing himself to be ready for anything, Alex was more nervous than he had been the day he'd auditioned for Juilliard. His hands trembled incessantly. His mouth felt completely parched, tongue clinging to the roof of his mouth and refusing to let go. Every time he tried to swallow it felt like he'd sucked down a walnut. And for what? Where did this stupid nervousness come from? It wasn't like Augusto meant anything to him. They weren't together and wouldn't be together. Augusto didn't matter and Alex had made an absolutely idiotic mistake coming out tonight. He just needed to go back home.

"Alex." Carolynne nudged him. "Give the man your ID."

"Oh. Sorry," Alex choked, digging in his back pocket for his identification. His hand shook so badly he could barely hold it still. Both Carolynne and the bouncer eyed him hard. "Too much coffee," he lied.

He put his card back in his pocket and slipped through the doors with Carolynne. Luckily, they'd missed the brunt of the crowd. The line behind them was long as hell and if Alex had waited outside any longer, he would've lost his nerve.

"Grab a table. I'll get our drinks," Carolynne ordered. Alex couldn't do much more than nod. Even though he'd been in Santo's once before, now it felt like walking on hallowed ground, or like blindly walking into enemy territory.

Alex grabbed a spot close to the stage, but not so close that if the lights somehow bled into the crowd, Augusto would see him. The last thing he wanted was for Augusto to think him a stalker or to mess up his routine just because Carolynne thought coming to the show would be hilarious. Right now, hilarity was far from accurate. Humility sounded more like it.

She returned with two Apple Martinis and slid one in front of Alex. He lifted it to his lips, again, hand shaking so badly the neon green liquid splashed around in the glass.

"Okay, what gives?" Carolynne asked, crossing her arms over her chest and eyeing him as if he were keeping some huge secret.

"Nothing," he lied again.

"Stop that. Something's wrong with you. Where's all your calm, cool, cocky charisma?"

"I'm not feeling so charismatic at the moment." And before she could rail him with a round of twenty questions, the music cranked up, smoke filled the room and the stage lights flared to life.

A line of men entered from downstage center. None of them were Augusto. The men walked slowly to the front of the stage dressed in nothing but leather pants. They were muscular but not the disgustingly huge kind. Music poured into the elegantly decorated room from every corner, embracing the crowd and the dancers, filling the air with a pulsing, primal-like rhythm. It excited Alex just a little bit, maybe more than he would've liked to admit.

The men slowly broke away and moved to the slow, deliberate beats of Madonna's *Human Nature*. One man, with brown hair and a mask covering his face was standing still while the others danced. Suddenly they all stopped and turned to face the dancer, frozen in the center of the stage.

I'm not sorry!

With those words, the statue of a man seemed to glide to the side exposing Augusto, dressed in the same leather pants, except he was sitting on a chair, his hands bound behind his back and he was blindfolded. His body rolled beautifully, like a belly dancer from one side to the other, before his head slipped back. He arched upward, his ass lifted from the seat only to hit it again when the beat became harsh. Alex could see the very breath he took when his lips parted slightly in a frozen scream of pleasure.

In that moment, Alex would've sworn he'd died and gone to heaven, or judging by the new tightness in his pants, this was hell. He sucked back damn near all his martini, then dragged his hand down his face. When he looked over, he found Carolynne, eyeballs nearly bursting from her skull, completely engrossed in the show.

Thank God for small miracles, he thought as he reached down to adjust himself, eyes rolling back as the welcome pressure pushed against his stiffening shaft. It took everything he had not to fall into the memory of their lips and bodies touching, not to give in to the desire and make an utter ass of himself. He was stronger than that, had more willpower than that and he was definitely better than that. Alex opened his eyes just in time to catch Augusto slamming his hips forward, and the sight of his body moving so carnally did nothing to restrain Alex's libido.

This is getting ridiculous. Something has to give.

It was all because of that damn kiss.

Augusto's body moved fluidly from one sensual move to another. The other men had their hands all over him. At the end of the first song he was still restrained while they moved him like a puppet, pulling his legs apart and closed. They manipulated his legs open once more and this time a blond dancer pressed his cheek against Augusto's knee and shoved his face upward, almost to his crotch, before spinning away. The routine ripened with sex but didn't quite get around to being overtly vulgar. It was sensual, intriguing, perfectly choreographed. Every breath measured, every dance step had heart and true emotions in it.

The lull between songs cast a raw energy through the club. Augusto was posed, legs planted on the stage, ass upward with his back bracing to the headrest of the chair. The second song, Michael Jackson's *Give in to Me*, was even sexier than before. In this one, Augusto was the dominant and led the group in a routine that carried the dancers off the stage gyrating and grinding with audience members.

One of the dancers, one far less impressive than Augusto, stalked right up to Alex and sat down in his lap as if there'd been an open invitation written on Alex's face. If there was, it'd had been meant for Augusto, not for any of the other far less talented, far less beautiful men who surrounded him. He would've much rather had the sexy Latino dancer from school grinding against his lap, but all that had to remain a fantasy.

Regardless though, Alex looked up at the stage and he could've sworn he caught Augusto spying him, watching what the other dancer was doing to him. And something wicked passed through Alex's thoughts. Augusto had never seen him move, and time had proven more than once that a man with the right moves could always get the man he wanted. He hoped this time it would pay off.

Alex gripped the sides of the chair and pushed upward, rolling his hips against the other dancer's ass. His strong legs held the weight of both their bodies, even though he knew better than to put any pressure on his foot. He didn't care right now. He only cared about the man on stage. He wanted his fantasy to see exactly what he was made of, that he had the same spice and sensuality Augusto did.

Arching his spine, Alex raised himself farther off the chair, head hanging over the back to expose the slender column of his neck. The man on top of him rolled, their groins meeting in a heated press. Alex felt the rawness and passion, though he dreamed of only one man being the one grinding against him and knotting his hair.

Augusto stood alone on the stage and for a while his routine didn't bring him to even turn in Alex's direction. The blindfold was gone and he was no longer tied up, but that didn't mean he was any less sexy than before. Suddenly, he looked straight over at Alex. Their eyes met and for a moment, neither man blinked. As though in slow motion, Augusto slicked his hair back just as the men switched positions and a new dancer ground against Alex.

The slow deliberate movements carried them through another song, one Alex had never heard before but found as equally erotic as the ones before it. He found himself pinned between two men now, standing and swaying with the rhythm of their bodies. He had his arm around one's neck while the other held onto his hips. Alex felt an impressive bulge against his ass and one at his groin, heard Carolynne catcalling over the music, but none of it mattered because none of them were the one he wanted to be close to.

CHAPTER SEVENTEEN

The show finally ended and after accepting a hug and a quick kiss to the side of the head from Luther, Augusto laughed and caught Keith and Jason to his chest, one in each arm.

"Oh! My! Gosh! That was amazing!" Jason cheered. "And those hips do *not* lie!"

Augusto laughed. "I take it you enjoyed the show?"

"Enjoy it?" Keith asked. "I have a hard-on and I'm not even into that whole blindfold-me-thing."

Augusto shook his head but couldn't stop grinning. A good performance always made him feel as if he was on top of the world. Then the thought of Alexander grinding on some random dancer hit him again and he felt physically ill.

"Hey, Gus! We're going to sit around and have a couple a beers after the club clears out later. Wanna stick around?" Chet called, poking his head through the door. "Say yes."

"Sure, Chet. I'll hang around for a bit."

"I'm coming to help you guys," Keith said and after patting Augusto on the shoulder, he left with Chet.

"All right, why do you look like someone peed in your coffee?" Jason asked, sitting in one of the other dancer's chairs.

The others were all missing because they tended to hang around the club, dancing with the patrons. Augusto never liked any of that stuff. And besides, the less chance he gave himself to get injured by some drunken moron, the better.

"What do you mean?"

"Come off it, Gus. I saw you when you walked in here and when you got on that stage. You had this—this air about you. Now you look like shit."

"It's nothing. I just need some air."

"Are you lying to me or yourself?" Jason tossed at Augusto's retreating back.

Those words stuck to him and even after he passed the guard and dipped outside, he knew Jason was right. Something was wrong. He was jealous. Before Alexander, it could have been argued there wasn't an envious bone in Augusto's body. That feeling should be proof enough he couldn't be with Alexander. Augusto, being the selfish kind when it came to his man, never wanted to share.

Alexander looked like the *sharing* kind.

Pressing his back against the wall, he rested his head on the rough brick, closed his eyes and inhaled greedily. The temperature had dropped a little and he was thankful. It cooled the heat within him, slowed his heart to a somewhat normal rhythm and gave him a chance to think straight.

Voices to his right caught his attention and he turned. He saw nothing but when he took a few steps and peeked around the bend, there stood Alexander sucking in air as though someone had told him the world was ending.

"What's wrong with you?" Augusto questioned.

"My foot is killing me," Alex said, voice painfully monotone. He didn't even raise his head. "Carolynne talked me into this, said it would be fun, said I didn't need the damn boot. It wasn't fun. Now my foot hurts." He finally glanced over. The pained expression on his face softened significantly. "You looked great up there."

"Thanks. You shouldn't be standing on that." Augusto wrapped an arm around Alexander's hips and pulled slightly. "Come inside."

"I don't want to go back inside yet," Alex admitted.

Rejected.

The lonely feeling of Alex's refusal lingered within Augusto like a bad taste. It shouldn't have hurt. But it did. Augusto took a step away from Alexander.

"I…I just need a minute," Alex added, easing out of Augusto's hold. He leaned back against the wall, but Augusto didn't leave him. Minutes of uncomfortable silence filled the air between them. Alex was the one who finally broke the verbal dry spell. "I couldn't stop watching you, the way you moved. I…I genuinely envied you."

"Jealous of me? It was a stage at Santo's, Alexander. Not Carnegie Hall."

"Maybe it's more appropriate to say I was jealous of the men dancing with you…"

"Funny. Seems you were the one bearing the brunt of the fun tonight."

Alex's head swung in Augusto's direction. He raked his fingers through his hair. That pained look appeared in his eyes again. "That was all about you," he said, voice low and somehow hurt. "I wanted you to see I could move too."

Augusto folded his arms over his chest. "I don't get you. One day you're treating me like scum, the next you want me to kiss you, then you're asking me why I'm even around and now—you think I rejected you so you want to show me that you can grind on some other guy? Well, good for you. Congratulations. Now I know. I have to go back inside."

"It wasn't some other guy," Alex called out, stopping Augusto before the door slammed between their conversation. "I was watching *you*. I was imagining *you*. I haven't stopped thinking about *you*. It has been about *you* since that first day in the private room."

Those words hit Augusto as if he was being punched in the gut. Each time Alexander said *you* Augusto winced, hoping not visibly, and turned his head away. "Why are you telling me all of this?" he questioned, voice raspy with arousal and pain. "Why?"

"Because I realized I need you. I don't know why or how, but I do. I'm attracted to you, sure. I loved kissing you." There was a pause, and Augusto had to force himself not to look over at Alex. He wouldn't give Alex the satisfaction, not if he could help it.

"God, did I love kissing you," Alex finally continued. "But there's never been a single time in my life that a kiss kept me this wrapped up in someone. I don't know, man. I don't know why I'm telling you, but it feels damn good to finally get it off my chest."

"I don't know what you want me to say to that." Augusto exhaled and turned to face Alex. "I mean you're unlike anyone I've ever been with or can see myself with. I can't deal with your life and the pettiness and—Alexander, you're who you are and it's not your fault. But I…I know you think you need me, but you can't need me and I don't want to be *just* wanted. I've had a taste of what it feels like to have a man go primal over me and my body and I can't go back to flights of fancy."

"So, I um…I guess that's where we stand." Alex shrugged. Augusto could've sworn he saw a little sadness glisten in Alex's eyes. "I guess I'll see you at school on Monday."

"That didn't end well," Augusto said softly, watching Alexander hobble off. It wasn't like he wanted to push Alexander away from him, but anything sexual between them would only break both their hearts. Alexander was not husband material, for he didn't seem to want to grow up. Everything was a game to him. He had to be the best at everything, but seemed obsessed with having everyone beneath him at all times. The man had no humility and Augusto needed that in a man.

Shit. Shit. Shit.

He walked back into the club and remained by himself until the place emptied out. Then he sat around with his friends, sipping on the same beer he had since the little get together began. While they talked and joked around, Augusto just couldn't get into it. He would chuckle from time to time but it wasn't as good as it should have been.

"You know what your problem is?" Chet questioned suddenly.

"No. I'm sure you're going to tell me." Augusto lifted his beer to his lips and took a long swig.

"You're too serious. You need to get laid." Chet nodded emphatically. "That would cure all that ails you."

"Oh please. Having sex doesn't solve anything." Augusto eased back in his seat. "Or rather it doesn't solve everything but one thing."

"You don't know what you're missing," Chet continued. "A good fuck solves everything."

Augusto crinkled his nose. "It never worked for me."

"That's because you're doing it wrong," Keith added.

"*Et tu*, Brutus?" Augusto moaned.

The group laughed.

"Look, all I'm saying is it's been a while for you and we want to see you happy." Keith put his bottle on the table and leaned in like a wise man ready to impart wisdom. "I know you, Gus. You think too much sometimes. You want love and I get that. You won't settle for just about anything or anyone and I get that too. But sometimes I think the man we're both looking for is not out there."

"What kind of man are we talking about?" Chet asked.

Before he could speak, Keith answered for him. "He wants a man that's true, strong, smart—not necessarily street smart but can hold a conversation without us wanting to stab him in the eyes with a spork."

Chet laughed. Augusto wanted to slam his head into the table.

"And how do you know that?" he questioned Keith.

"Because I know you and any man you end up being with cannot be a creeper. He has to have a good heart to match his good looks."

Augusto bowed his head and took another long drink from his beer. "Well, shit. It seems I'm looking for a saint."

"And that's not a bad thing," Chet said softly.

"Yo! Augusto!"

That voice. It couldn't be. It was way too late for a visitor.

For a moment, Augusto remained frozen, fingers tightening around the bottle. He couldn't have heard what he thought he did. The others were all looking behind him and he knew he hadn't been imagining it. Augusto swung around. His heart raced, his knees wobbled and his beer hit the ground. The glass broke, sending liquid all over his feet but he didn't care. He jerked up from his seat and stood behind it, staring at the large black man walking toward him with the widest smile he'd ever seen.

"Donny! *Yo no creí que volvería!*" Augusto's voice cracked.

"La guerra no podía sostenerme!"

He rushed forward and stood before Donny, cradling his face for a moment. When his gaze blurred with tears, Augusto hugged Donny tightly and was squeezed back in return. Donny kissed the side of his head before pushing him back slightly to look him over, only to hug him again. *"Te extrañé."*

"I missed you, too. We can talk later." Donny turned to greet the others with bumped fists.

Donny walked away with Augusto and they sat at a table together. Augusto took a breath. He looked over at Donny, noticing the scar against the left side of his face and winced. "That's new," he said in Spanish. "What happened?"

"Roadside bomb," Donny whispered. "I lost a couple of men in it. I got hurt."

"That's why I haven't heard from you in about two weeks?"

Donny nodded. "I didn't mean to worry you."

"Did you tell Mammie?" Augusto asked.

"No. I don't think her heart could take missing a son."

Augusto made a face. "But you're not missing."

"That's not the point." Donny sighed. "I was hurt real bad, Gus. She would've worried and then used her life savings to rush to Germany to spend every waking moment at my bedside—you know Mammie as well as I do. I wouldn't be able to live with that."

Augusto didn't understand not telling Mammie. The truth was he didn't understand anything about war—about giving up everything to serve a country. But he knew it all made sense to Donny and that was perfect for him. "Okay, bro. I get it."

"You don't." Donny laughed. "I can see it in your eyes. But it's all good. How have you been?"

"I got into Julliard."

"No!" Donny cheered. "Congratulations! How do you like it?"

"As much as one can like having their dick chopped off on a daily basis." Augusto managed a smile.

Donny grinned. "Now who's being dramatic? You can do this. They wouldn't have accepted you if they didn't think you would be a shining example of excellence."

"You're my brother. You have to say that."

Donny shrugged. "That's true too. But you're forgetting, I've seen you dance. I've seen you do things that moved Mammie to tears and she doesn't even like Krumping. So whenever you feel you're not good enough—just remember that."

Augusto nodded.

"So, you seeing anyone?"

"No," Augusto replied. His mind rushed to Alex but he didn't know if that could be considered *seeing* someone.

"Bro, it's been years…"

"I know, Don. I get it. I just have to find the right man."

"Let me give you some advice, huh?" Donny leaned in. "Don't sit back and say you're looking for the perfect man—another Kemar. I adored the man too but there will never be another him. Sure, there might be someone with his attributes but the way your heart felt about him cannot be duplicated. Find someone who adores you and work on it."

Augusto took a breath. The truth was he had been looking

for another Kemar—seeing if he could see Kemar's face in the eyes of all the men who flirted with him. But so far they were all duds, even Alexander.

"Listen," Donny interrupted his thoughts. "I have to go for a bit. You wanna come by the house a little later? I know it's late but I'm going to see Mammie because you know what'll happen if I don't."

"All right, man." The two bumped fists, hugged and Augusto watched Donny leave before joining his friends again. When he sat down he was pretty sure there was no measure for the happiness he was feeling at that precise moment.

CHAPTER EIGHTEEN

Alex's foot hadn't stopped throbbing, despite the pain pills, despite the booze, despite the long hot soak in the tub. He suspected it had more to do with the all over ache he felt than it had to do with the ridiculous injury he'd gotten more than three weeks ago while practicing for a part he obviously wouldn't get now.

Cheek pressed against the cold porcelain on the side wall of the tub, Alex groaned hard and loud, misery echoing back at him and plowing right into his eardrums. He rolled from his side, onto his back, sinking further into the water as he silently cursed himself for walking away from Augusto last night. What else could he have done though? Augusto had made it very, very clear he didn't want anything to do with Alex. Abundantly clear. The fact didn't keep Alex from wanting him though, and wanting Augusto had prevented Alex from sleeping last night.

And there he was, a whole twelve hours later, still reeling over everything that had happened between them.

Maybe Augusto had been right. Maybe Alex was selfish and self-absorbed. Maybe he didn't deserve to be happy because he treated everyone around him like shit. The thought hurt, genuinely, all the way down to the very center of his being. So now, instead of thoughts of Augusto turning him on, they made him feel like a small, insignificant waste of air.

"Alex? You in here?" he heard Kenneth calling from somewhere outside the bathroom door.

Slipping further down in the giant tub, Alex considered keeping his trap shut so Kenneth would go away, but that would make him an even bigger asshole. Just because he lusted after someone else, he was going to turn away the only man who seemed to live and breathe for him?

Genius, Alex, you have it.

"I'm in the tub," he said with a loud sigh.

"Can I come in?"

No. "Yes." The door slowly opened and his sexy bad boy peeked his head in through the crack. Alex nodded him over. "You're a sight for sore eyes."

"You look like hell," Kenneth countered.

The moment Kenneth fully breached the door, Alex's heart started its descent inside his chest. For the first time since meeting his hunk of burning lust, Alex didn't look at Kenneth and immediately want him pressed against his backside. Quite the opposite in fact. He barely wanted Kenneth to see him naked right now. It felt dishonest. As if he were somehow cheating on Augusto, even though Augusto didn't want anything to do with him.

Kenneth stood in the center of the bathroom, hands buried deep in his pockets. The uncomfortable silence that seemed to be following Alex around these days wedged its intangible self right between them. Kenneth's stare bounced around the room. Alex couldn't bring himself to look directly at the man he'd been messing around with part-time since he'd come to Juilliard last year.

"So, Carolynne said you guys had fun at Santo's," Kenneth murmured.

"I suppose. Did she tell you about me dancing?"

The edge of Kenneth's lips crooked upward. "Yeah. Said it was hot. Kinda hate that I missed it."

"You're not mad?"

"No. Do I have a right to be?"

"Kenneth, I did a very sexual dance with two men who I don't know. We've been fucking for how long now? Are you hurt? Are you upset with me?"

"Not really."

That two word response was like a blinding light bulb coming on in Alex's head. While he'd known he never loved and *would* never love Kenneth, his lover *not* being angry made what Augusto had said last night even more painful than it had been when he'd been staring into Augusto's big brown eyes. Alex *was* just a whore. Nothing more. Nothing less. Unworthy of love, but worst of all, unworthy of Augusto's love. The same had been true of every lover Alex had ever had, even the one he'd come the closest to caring about—Ross, a married man who had a proclivity for young men, a man who'd kept Alex his dirty little secret from a wife who loved money more than she loved her husband, a man who would never own his sexuality and truly be with Alex the way Alex had wanted him to.

Kenneth reached down and gripped the hem of his T-shirt. He started to lift it over his head when Alex stopped him by asking, "What are you doing?"

"Getting naked."

"Why?"

"Because you're naked."

"Is that really all we are to each other, Kenny? Just lovers? Are we not even friends?"

Kenny shrugged. "We don't have anything in common. We don't talk or spend time with each other. We don't go on dates. What else would we be?"

"I don't know," Alex quietly, painfully admitted. "Keep your clothes on."

"Are you mad at me?"

"No, I'm mad at myself," Alex said as he eased up from the quickly cooling water of the bath he'd spent way too much time in.

Just so he wouldn't have to look at Kenny's beautifully tragic frowning face, Alex turned his gaze down to his wrinkled hands. He stood naked and not the least bit turned on. Kenneth wasn't rushing to be close to him either.

"I think I'm going to go back to bed," Alex said, voice as

somber as his demeanor. "I'll call you when I wake up again."

"Should I send Carolynne over?"

"No, I'm just…" He sighed heavily, then finally looked back up to find Kenneth staring at him. "I'm just going to go back to bed."

Normally, they would've kissed, hugged or touched each other before parting ways, not a gesture of love but more a gesture of caring. Alex did care about Kenny. Their feelings just fell very short of anything resembling love.

"I guess I'll see you later then," Kenneth finally said.

"Sure. Later."

With that, Kenneth left the bathroom, leaving Alex alone and seriously falling apart on the inside. Maybe if Kenneth played hard to get like Augusto did, Alex would've felt something more. Maybe he wouldn't have. Who knows?

He wrapped a towel around his waist, then padded out into his apartment. He felt so lost now that he wasn't sure what to do. Going back to bed had been an excuse to get rid of Kenneth. He couldn't sleep right now if he tried. So, he headed on into the kitchen, thinking he might eat, but the fridge was just as depressing—all bare and empty save for a few cartons of leftover takeout.

Alex slammed the refrigerator door shut with disgust, then hobbled toward his bedroom. Maybe he should just stay in bed all day, avoid the phone, avoid company, avoid anything that might remind him of what a miserable piece of crap he apparently was.

CHAPTER NINETEEN

Sunday found Augusto sitting beneath the large tree in his mother's backyard with his back against the trunk, a cold beer in his hand, his mother shelling peas from the husk at the garden table and Donny's head in his lap. He missed these lazy Sundays. Growing up he'd looked forward to them for his weeks were always hectic—sometimes more than a child should have to go through.

Today, he spent the majority of their get-together rehashing the story about Alexander. At the end of the tale, he drained his beer in one drink.

"Maybe you're being too hard on him," Donny said, shifting against Augusto's thigh. "Maybe being a jerk is all he's ever known because he's had to use it to prop himself up his whole life."

"Who knows?" His mother chimed in, speaking Spanish. "Maybe his parents are jerks. They always say the apple doesn't fall far from the tree."

Augusto thought over what they were saying but he just couldn't let his himself get caught up with Alexander and wind up sorry for it later. But what kind of life would that be? And what kind of life could he have with Alexander?

"Maybe I'm too young to be thinking of another relationship so seriously. Pass me another beer, would you?"

Donny handed him another bottle. "What do you mean?"

"Thanks." He wrung the cap from the cold bottle. "I was with Kemar for a while. We were so serious he was thinking of marriage. Maybe that one time, and that close call was all I was meant to have. Maybe I should live a little. Sow my wild oats as it were."

Donny laughed. He laughed so hard he rolled from side to side. Mammie wasn't impressed by that suggestion one bit and glared at both him and Donny. She arched a brow before pointing an accusatory finger at him. Growing up as a kid, when that finger came up, it was the first sign he was in trouble.

"Augusto Rafael Catalan!" She called.

Shit! My whole name! Second sign I'm in trouble.

"None of that talk. I raised you better than that. If you like this boy, then do something about it. Maybe he will change when he sees how important certain things are to you."

"But, Mammie, Alexander can't love anyone else but himself."

"That's not true." She put the finger away. "Everyone is capable of loving someone else. It may not be to the same degree we'd like, but they are capable. We have to believe that. Maybe you just have to show him some kindness."

"Well, I have an idea," Donny said, sitting up and grabbing his own beer from the cooler. "Why don't you invite him out to go dancing with you? Not you on a stage and him grinding with other men. You and him together on the dance floor. Maybe that could put some things in perspective for the both of you."

"He can't dance right now. He injured his foot."

Donny sighed and then took a drink. "Well, hell," he muttered.

Augusto pushed himself off the tree then approached his mother. He sat across from her, quietly helping her remove the tiny peas from the pods. He said nothing and silence swept over the backyard, leaving the sound of leaves even more intoxicating. Breathing was easy at his mother's place, away from the city noise and pretense. It was far away from the pain he felt whenever he saw Alexander.

"*Escucha me*, Gusie," Mammie began. "I adore you, you know that, right?"

"I know, Mammie."

"And when you told me you were gay I thought your life was over. Being gay was all over the news with them debating if gays should marry and what their rights were and I never wanted you to end up alone. If they hadn't legalized gay marriage…" Her voice caught, cracked and trailed off. He saw tears in her eyes and kissed her forehead then her cheek. "Then I saw how happy you and Kemar were together. Suddenly it didn't matter if you could get married because I knew that boy loved you. He would get this big grin on his face when you walked into a room and that was only a look of a man who was deeply, deeply in love. And your smile—that's all a mother truly wants for her children, you know? Happiness. Right now, Gus, you aren't happy."

"And you think Alexander will make me happy?"

"I can't answer that for you. What I can tell you is this: there's a battle being waged between what you think is right and opposite that is Alexander's personality. Maybe what the two of you need is time away together to see if this is what you both want. Normally, I wouldn't suggest this yet but I know you, Gussie. You're going to spend your whole time obsessing over this until you make yourself sick or drive yourself and us crazy." She stopped speaking for a moment, looking thoughtful. "Okay, so here's what I'm going to suggest. Your Gram's house is still there in Finger Lakes. I find it's a wonderful place to go when you need to find yourself. I'm sure it'll work miracles for what's happening between yourself and Alexander. Why not take him there and see what happens? They give you a spring break at that fancy school of yours, don't they?"

Augusto smiled at her. "Yes, they do."

"Good. I don't know how your money situation is but you can ask him to go with you. Explain to him you couldn't pay for him to get there but his food and a place to stay will be taken care of. And spend the week getting to know him outside of all the fancy and the noise."

"It's a good idea, Mammie, but I don't think he would like that." Augusto glanced at his watch and took a breath.

"And why not?"

"Because—he's more of a five star, Ritz-Carlton kind of guy."

"Take a chance, Gus."

"I really have to go, Mammie. I'll come back the first chance I get, okay?" He hugged her tightly. "Donny, wanna give me a ride to the Greyhound?"

"Yeah, sure. Lemme pee first."

Augusto made a face and their mother tossed a pea at Donny who merely laughed and dodged it quite easily.

"When your father and I adopted Donny, it was because we loved him and we thought he would make a wonderful brother to you. We couldn't have any more children, he needed a home and a family. He is your family, *mi hijo*. He has wide shoulders. Lean on them."

Augusto smiled. He kissed her cheek and hugged her one more time. "I love you, Mammie."

"*Te amo tambien.*"

The ride to the bus was quiet except when Donny forced him to say something. Then, it always went back to Augusto's classes and what he wanted to do after school. After all he was a dancer and should be thinking at least five years ahead for some strange reason. Augusto wasn't sure—that was the final consensus.

"I'm such a jerk," Augusto moaned. "All this talk has been about me. I forgot to ask about you. What are you going to do now that you're finished with the military?"

"Me? I want to start my own security firm. I have a couple of guys who want in and I know I could get a small loan from the bank to help me start off. I met a prince from Saudi Arabia when I was on leave in Germany who asked if I was willing to help with the detail on his son when he is here for college next year."

"You said yes, right?"

"I said I would think about it. I wasn't sure I was coming home sometimes. But now that I'm here, I can actually call him up and say yes. But I wanted to wait until after I got something off the ground."

"Good plan."

At the bus terminal, Donny turned in his seat to hug him. "And don't worry about this Alexander thing. These things have a way of working themselves out."

Augusto thanked him and scrambled from the car. He threw his bag over his shoulder, stuck his music in his ears and made his way into the terminal. If he was lucky he would be back home before it got too dark outside.

CHAPTER TWENTY

The classroom was completely empty Monday morning. As well it should've been. Students weren't due to arrive for another hour. Madame Margot had called in feeling a bit under the weather, so the note left on her desk said, and she'd decided to stay away from the young dancers so her sickness didn't jeopardize their health. She was caring like that. Compassionate.

Alex sat behind her desk with one long, slim leg drawn up to his chest. He stared down at three white pieces of paper. During his battle with insomnia the night before he'd come up with an absolutely brilliant plan to win Augusto over, or if nothing else, show him that he wasn't a complete monster, even if there was some truth to that thought. Alex sincerely hoped the "gifts"— for lack of a better word—appealed to the dancer's cultured side.

The ticking of the clock on the far wall was almost maddening. It felt a lot like waiting for a judge to decide Alex's fate. If things went as he hoped, this valiant gesture wouldn't turn out to be a complete flop and he wouldn't make an enemy out of the man he desired so much. Then again, Augusto could take it as a slap in the face. And with that thought, he prayed for Augusto to walk through the door first so no one else could possibly witness Alex's utter demise.

He raised his head when he heard the knob jiggle. His silent prayers turned even more desperate, and as if God had been listening, Augusto walked through the door.

Thank you!

They exchanged a quick glance then immediately looked away from each other. Now that he had Augusto alone, Alex wasn't sure where to begin.

"About the other night—"

"Don't worry about it," Augusto replied, dropping his bag in the corner. "I shouldn't have been so hard on you."

"No. I'm glad you were. I've been doing a lot of thinking." *No sleeping really.* "You're right about me and I deserved every word you said. I want to change though. Do you think people can change?"

"My mom seems to think so." August leaned into the wall and crossed his arms over his chest.

"But what do *you* think? Do you think a self-centered asshole can become a nice guy?"

Augusto's eyes became weary. "I don't know, Alexander. I suppose if this ass wanted to change bad enough. Let's say, he finds something he believes worthy enough to make him a better person, then yes."

"Then maybe there's hope for me."

Alex stood from the chair behind their teacher's desk, grabbing the three slips of paper on his way toward Augusto. It was do or die now. Time to dive in and hope he didn't sink.

He held up the first piece of paper, and said, "This is a ticket to *Stomp* on Broadway." Then the second slip. "Before you tell me you have nothing to wear, this is a tuxedo rental." Lastly, he held up the final piece to his romantic puzzle. "This is the number for my father's car service. If you choose to go, call this number and they'll send a sedan to pick you up."

"Alexander, I—"

Holding up one hand to stop Augusto from arguing, he said, "This can be a date if you want. Or it can be two friends catching a great show. Then again, it can be nothing more than a token of appreciation. That's up to you." Alex inhaled sharply then slowly let it go. "You can decide to go or not. If you do, then I'll know I didn't completely ruin my chances with you. If you don't show, then you won't have to worry about me chasing after you anymore. I'll know my place and I'll back off."

Alexander could already see the wheels of contemplation running rampant in Augusto's head. The Latino dancer opened his mouth to say something, but probably thought better of it for he said nothing for a while. He merely held the papers he was given, staring down at them. When he finally lifted his head, his eyes were unreadable.

"So, I don't have to make this decision now." It was more of a statement than a question.

"No. The show isn't until Friday."

"All right. I'll let you know."

Augusto turned his back and started toward the center barre. Alex could hear voices getting closer just outside the door. He wasn't ready for this to be over yet, even though he had a good feeling it was.

"Hey, Augusto?"

"Mhmm?"

"Please be there." Those were the last words he uttered before the room filled with other students.

Alex had thought that doing this would've made him feel a whole lot better, but it didn't. Now he had to wait until Friday night to see if Augusto was genuinely interested or if he was completely out of the game on this one. He hoped the latter wasn't the case. He hadn't done anything like this for anyone else in his whole life. If that wasn't an admittance of real feelings, then what the hell was?

Chapter Twenty-one

Class was the break he needed from what happened between himself and Alexander at the beginning of it. Having Alexander overseeing the class was another form of hell for him, still, he toughed it out. But by the time it was finished and he'd showered, Augusto had to run to make it to his next class on time with the tickets burning a hole in his bag. The day slipped by and he went out of his way not to see Alexander. He walked down a different set of corridors, bypassed the elevators all together and took the stairs. When classes ended Jason ambushed him on his way to the subway.

"Are you going to tell me what's up with Alexander Benton?"

"What do you mean?"

"What I mean is he's actually acting human," Jason said. "And to scare me even more? I passed him in the hall and he said *hey*."

Augusto shoved his fingers into his pockets and shrugged. "He seems to think I'm the man of his dreams."

"I'm sorry. What?"

"You heard me."

Jason hurried forward then walked backward so he could face Augusto. "But you're not so sure?"

"Precisely." Augusto stepped around his friend as they fell into step beside each other once more. "I mean, how would you like it if someone came to you and asked you what is up with your man then followed it up by *'he's acting human'*? I don't want a man who's cruel to people. But Mammie said I'm being too tough on him."

"True. You can't hold the wealthy up to the same standards we do ourselves. They don't really have to have self-control or even dignity. They have the one thing the rest of us don't…money."

"He asked me out Friday night."

"And?"

"And what?"

"Gus! Are you going?"

"I don't know."

"You have to work?" Jason questioned.

"No. Chet is leading that night since I have tests coming up."

"Then why aren't you going?" Jason sounded confused. "I know he's a bit of a jerk but you can't still think this is a practical joke."

"I think it is. I mean, the first day I showed up here he started in on me. And I know he said he needed me and that me rejecting him hurt but—damn! I don't know what to think now."

"So you'd rather settle on the Carrie scenario? If he pulls anything like that have Donny and some of his muscular, military buddies kick his skinny ass. That would make you feel better."

Augusto laughed and stopped in front of the subway. "I'll talk to you later."

At home the apartment was nice and cool. Keith was there with a bunch of his Police Foundation buddies, some of which Augusto prayed would never get to carry a weapon. Their obsession with guns scared Augusto but he never mentioned it to Keith. When he walked in they all turned, raised their glasses to him and screamed his name. Augusto laughed and stopped to greet them all and after a quick snack from Keith's plate of fries and wings, he excused himself and locked the door to his room. The stinking dog was barking again but this time not as bad. The AC worked and for some reason, that made everything okay. Instead of screaming at the dog and its owner again, Augusto closed the window and yanked the curtains closed. He picked up his guitar and began playing slowly. He thought of Alexander and the decision he had to make. It shouldn't be so complicated but his mother and brother made some sense about giving Alexander a chance. Then again, he wasn't entirely sure if he wanted to do that in a hired car and a penguin suit.

He stopped playing and pressed his palm over the vibrating strings to silence them. His head was starting to throb.

Whenever his migraines hit a shower normally helped. Augusto took a moment to stash the guitar back in its case then snuck down the hall for a shower. Since none of Keith's friends knew the word *knock* he locked the door and stripped. The water flowed over his head, soaking through his hair and soon it wasn't water anymore but Alexander's hands. Augusto pressed his eyes closed and allowed the fantasy to overwhelm him. With his chest rising and falling, he looked down and noticed his cock had swollen to full arousal; with each thought of Alexander's lips on his, the hardened muscled jerked up and down.

"Damn."

All through the shower he was heavily aroused. Putting clothes on was a chore, for the moment his cock rubbed the material of his boxers, all Augusto wanted to do was find Alexander and take what his body so desperately craved. But he had to behave. Seeing Alexander every day tortured him enough. He didn't want to add awkward to it. Every time their eyes met across a room or they brushed by each other in the halls muttering the faintest of apologies, Augusto's body jerked to attention, sending his heart into a tailspin.

Every day since Alexander's offer, Augusto had gone out of his way not to go by Alexander any more than he had to. Suddenly Friday arrived and Augusto wasn't sure where the time had gone. To make matters worse, Augusto still hadn't made a decision about what to do with the tickets.

Everything seemed to go downhill the moment he woke up that morning. He was late for his first class and to compound the crappiness of the day, he saw Alexander with a group of his friends and froze. His legs would not obey his brain. Their eyes locked and for a moment, Augusto wasn't sure if he should say hello or just walk away.

The girl who always seemed to be by Alexander's side elbowed him. "Dude! You're zoning again—what's the matter with you?"

He turned back to her, ignoring Augusto's presence.

After those words and Alexander's reaction, Augusto broke the trance, raked his fingers through his hair and dipped down the stairs.

CHAPTER TWENTY-TWO

Never in his life had Alex felt out of place in a tuxedo, not like he did right now. The tie was way too tight. The vest hugged him so hard he could barely breathe. The pants were too high on his waist. Miserable. Absolutely miserable, and to top it all off, the show was completely sold out so the theater closely resembled a tin can packed with sardines. At least it did in his mind anyway. Truth be told, it was probably one of the nicest theaters on Broadway—grand and elegant, with rows of seats and balconies and curtains. Waiting in the lobby was the only bad part about it, but Alex refused to move from that spot until Augusto showed up or the ushers started closing the doors, whichever happened first.

He stood in the center of the room, rocking back and forth on the heels of the shiny designer shoes he only wore when he was forced into a tuxedo. He'd ditched the walking boot because this special occasion called for something so much classier than polyester, nylon and Velcro. Besides, the last thing he wanted was for Augusto to see him limping around in that oversized contraption.

Alex twirled a single yellow rose between his thumb and his forefinger. The stem had been cut short and wrapped in green tape. A pearled pin stuck to the side. It was identical to the one he wore on his lapel. He wanted there to be absolutely no doubt in anyone's mind that he and Augusto were together... if Augusto showed up.

"Curtain call. Fifteen minutes," the usher announced.

It was getting down to the wire and Alex's hope was land sliding into despair. He should've seen this coming. Augusto didn't want him and made no bones about making that fact very, very clear. Alex was stupid to get his hopes up in the first place.

Still, he couldn't help it. Augusto had to know how sincere he'd been. Weren't Alex's layers of bullshit thin enough for anyone paying any attention to see right through? Didn't he deserve a chance, even a small one? This wasn't some cheap date. It was well thought out, elaborate and very, very expensive.

See, that's your problem, Alex. You think money can buy you whatever you want. You think it can make people forget what an asshole you really are.

"Ten minutes to curtain call," the usher announced again. Every time Alex heard the man's voice his heart sunk a little deeper in his body.

Sighing, Alex raked his hand through his hair and dropped his gaze to the floor. His stare traced the gold and red patterns in the carpet because he couldn't make himself keep watching through the glass doors for someone who would never be there.

He knew the usher was about to call it, and for a moment he debated just leaving and drowning his sorrows in a good Riesling. Wine always made things better.

Without immediately raising his head, he started toward the door, watching all the shiny shoes race past him. He looked up so he wouldn't bump into anyone and that's when he saw Augusto watching him through the glass, more handsome than Alex had ever seen him, more debonair than he could've dreamed. The sight stole Alex's breath away and forced his lips into a relieved smile.

Augusto had his hands pressed to his sides and his hair slicked back. Even the way he moved was sexy and he wasn't even dancing. Finally, Augusto entered and stood before him silently, watching his face. "Hi."

"Hey," Alex responded in a breathy rush. "Didn't think you would make it."

"It was kind of a last minute deal." Augusto offered a small smile.

"Five minutes to curtain," the usher warned.

"Guess we should go in," Alex said. He was so nervous he'd forgotten about the yellow rose he'd been fidgeting with the whole time. He lifted the flower up and said, "I got you a boutonnière. May I pin it on you?"

Augusto nodded but his intense stare never left Alex, even as he took a step forward.

Alex's fingers shook as he carefully pinned the flower to Augusto's lapel. The last time he remembered being this nervous—in a good way—was the time he'd admitted to actually loving someone. That someone had ended up being the wrong man. Fortunately though, he realized it long ago and the knowledge left plenty of space in his heart for someone as good and sincere as Augusto seemed to be.

His hand lingered for a moment after settling the flower in place, only because he wanted to feel Augusto's heart pounding as hard as his. The notion was silly though, and Alex knew that, but he still had to give it a try.

"You ready?" he asked, holding his hand out for Augusto to take if he chose to.

Instead of answering, Augusto took his hand, wrapping long, strong fingers around his. Alex's shoulders rose and fell as though a weight lifted from them.

Together, they walked into the theater. His seats were first row, front and center on the balcony, great seats as long as they both had perfect vision. It really didn't matter much to Alex. He only cared about seeing the dancer beside him.

They took their seats and Alex didn't dare let go of Augusto's hand. He leaned over and said, "It's sacrilege to come to New York and not see a Broadway show, especially if you like musicals at all."

Augusto laughed softly. "You know, my mother said the same thing the day I took her to see *The Lion King*."

"So you've seen a Broadway show before?" Alex asked, surprise seeping into his voice. He cringed. How could he be so narrow-minded to assume Augusto hadn't? "I'm sorry, I…I'm an idiot. That's what I am. I assumed…" Alex bit his lip. "Just tell me to shut up before I make an even bigger ass of myself."

Shaking his head, Augusto leaned over and pressed a kiss to the side of Alexander's head. "It's fine. A lot of people don't think me particularly cultured. I mean the first time most of them ever see me I'm on stage at Santo's gyrating or something. But my brother and I went to see *La Bohème* two years ago. He was stationed in Italy. It took a lot of overtime but I made it happen."

"That must've been amazing."

As soon as music roared through the room and the house lights died down, Alex tightened his hand around Augusto's. It felt like the right thing to do because he didn't want to feel any other hand in his. His smile widened when he caught a glimpse of the stage lights sparkling in Augusto's big brown eyes. Euphoric.

CHAPTER TWENTY-THREE

Seeing *Stomp* a second time didn't make it any less magnificent. Augusto hadn't mentioned he'd already seen the show because Alexander seemed to be genuinely trying. True, him going was a last minute decision. But sitting on his bed a few years from now wondering *what if* would have driven him nuts. Alex's hand remained in his through the whole show, though he thought for sure Alex would have let go at some point. Instead, his fingers tightened around Augusto's.

He smiled in the semi-dark, feeling perfectly at ease the way they were sitting and from time to time he could tell Alexander was staring at him. At one point he smirked and without peeling his eyes from the stage, he leaned over. "Shouldn't you be watching the show?" he whispered.

"Would you believe me if I told you I was trying to?"

"Oh, not a chance."

Alexander gave a soft laugh and the warmest, sincerest smile Augusto had ever seen from him. The other man looked happy, genuinely happy. He said, "It's not my fault the view beside me is more mesmerizing than what's going on up on that stage."

"I bet you say that to all your dates." Augusto turned away but smiled. He hoped the theater was dark enough so Alexander didn't see the grin but he couldn't help the happiness coursing through him.

"Believe it or not, I don't date much," Alexander softly admitted. "It's been a long time since I cared enough…" His voice trailed off as he looked back to the stage, as if he had more to say but didn't want to share whatever it was right now.

Augusto stared at him for longer than he probably should have. When he finally turned back to the stage, it was because people around him were applauding. They rose to their feet so he followed, releasing Alexander's hand to join in the uproar.

He glanced at Alexander beside him, and right as the people sat again, he noticed a few making their way toward the door. He knew why—they wanted to make it out before the rush of everyone else. He grabbed Alexander's hand again.

"Come on," he said, tugging.

Before Alexander could utter a word, Augusto had him down the aisle and into the lobby. Augusto slowed down then, but didn't let go of Alexander's hand. It wasn't until Alexander turned to dead weight that Augusto stopped. He looked back and found the smile on Alexander's face hadn't just faded, but disappeared completely. His skin had turned pale white. His body had gone rigid. "Alex?"

Alexander quietly said, "Let's go," but before they could duck out, a woman in sequin formal wear called his name, heading toward him with outstretched arms.

"Alexander Benton? Is that you?"

She all but squealed as she pulled Alexander into her arms and held him tightly, hand wrapped around the back of his head. He didn't speak, only glared over her shoulder at the silver-haired man behind her.

Augusto watched the interaction between the three. Alexander had the look of tolerance for the woman—the one you gave an overbearing neighbor who was always happy to see you and delve into some long-winded conversation about the grandkids. But for the man, Alexander's expression was something else. The reaction reminded him of when he saw his mother's best friend's husband. The man gave him the creeps and always wanted to have conversations with him while undressing Augusto with his eyes. He stepped forward and took hold of Alex's hand, trying to pry him out of the woman's arms without being too obvious.

"We were kinda in a rush to leave," Augusto spoke, trying desperately not to be rude.

"I'm sorry. I…" The woman frowned at Alexander.

"I'm sorry, Marilyn," Alex said. "We have things scheduled at the school tomorrow and I need some rest. Rain check?"

"Sure." She stepped back and grabbed the older man's hand. "Ross and I will stop by and see your parents soon. How are they?"

"They're spending the summer in the Hamptons as always."

"We all need to get together soon."

"Sure. Just, um…call Mom. I'm sure she'd love to hear from you." Alex's jaw clenched tightly as he looked back to the man Augusto assumed was Ross. He cut his eyes away, then said, "We really need to go."

"It was good to see you again," Marilyn offered, nudging her husband's arm. "Right, Ross?"

Ross cleared his throat. "Right. Honey, let the boy go already."

Alexander nodded his head then spun on his heel.

Something was wrong. Augusto watched the way Ross eyed Alexander. He recognized that look. It was the same one Kemar had given him across the dinner table the first time Kemar took him home to meet Luther. It was before Kemar had told his father he was gay. It was the same lust-filled gaze that spoke of quiet, secret pleasures and silent yearning.

"I think I'm going to be sick," Augusto said, releasing Alexander's hand and brushing hard by Ross. His hand came up over his mouth and he made for the door.

"Augusto!" Alexander called out, chasing after him. They both charged through the crowd, knocking elbows with strangers. "Augusto, stop!"

But Augusto didn't stop. He couldn't face up to the realization that just slammed into him like a Mack Truck. He shouldered his way through the rest of the people blocking the door until he burst outside. Without looking, he charged across the street forcing a driver in a black Mercedes to slam on their brakes, leaving the tires squealing. Across the street he pressed his forehead into the wall and sucked in enough air to fill his lungs and burn. Alexander called his name and Augusto whirled around.

"Are you kidding me?" Augusto snapped. "Are you *fucking*

kidding me? Tell me it's not happening!"

"Whoa." Alexander stood back, eyes as wide as saucers. "What exactly do you think you saw in there?"

Augusto frowned. "I know you think I'm some ghetto boy but I'm not stupid. You and Ross."

"Yeah, me and Ross…ended two years ago." Alexander took a step closer. He lowered his head. Augusto noticed his Adam's apple bobbing in his throat. When Alex spoke again, there was a slight waver to his voice. "I was seventeen when we hooked up. That…asshole manipulated the fuck out of me. He told me he loved me. Said his wife knew he wasn't completely straight. I…" Alexander scrubbed his hands over his face as dragged in a few short breaths. "He…" He licked his lips then looked up at Augusto. "He broke my fucking heart. He broke *me*."

The anger mixed with adrenaline surged through him and Augusto helplessly bowed his head to press his forehead to Alexander's shoulder. He felt so sick with the whole idea. So many parts of him told him to be angry at Alexander, to be disgusted, but he just couldn't pull it out of himself. His ass hit the wall.

"I just…" he swallowed, wrapped his arms around Alexander's back and pulled him in.

"That wasn't supposed to happen," Alexander whispered, laying his head on Augusto's shoulder. "I know what you think. It wasn't like that with him. He was my first love and first heartbreak. I…I'm so sorry. I swear to God, I'll tell you everything, if you want to know. But it's not what you think. I didn't whore around with him."

Augusto winced and pulled from between the wall and Alexander's body. He grabbed his hair, pushing it from his face while looking up at the sky, wondering why this whole deal with Alexander was testing his patience so desperately. "You were seventeen. Why would you even go out with a man that age? You had to have known better."

"It was about the time I really admitted to myself I was gay. I mean, I knew, but I hadn't accepted it. I came out to him first

because I was terrified of telling my dad. Ross was there for me."
Alexander shrugged and shifted his weight from his bad foot.
"Ross talked me through it. Everything was innocent at first. He
said he knew it all along, then he told me his secret. He would
make excuses to take me out, just to do the normal shit my dad
wasn't around to do with me. Next thing I knew, he was kissing
me. The night of my eighteenth birthday he told me he loved me
and I said it back. I'd loved him far, *far* longer, but I was afraid of
pushing him away. I…hindsight is twenty-twenty, right? I haven't
been serious with anyone since."

"You were underage, Alexander. He had no right…" Stopping
himself from sending his blood pressure any higher, he took a
moment, breathing silently with the night air flowing through
him and caressing his skin. "And this—what we're doing here.
What's this?"

"The scariest thing I've done since," Alexander quietly
admitted. "The first time I've wanted something more than just
sex with someone since he…"

Augusto stepped closer then. He used his thumb and index
finger to lift Alexander's chin so their eyes could meet. "Since he
what?"

"Since he taught me how badly love really hurts."

"So you don't love him anymore…"

"No." Alexander shook his head, keeping his icy blue stare
trained on Augusto's eyes. "Haven't loved him for a long time.
Took about a year to stop loving him. Took longer to get over
him. The night he told his wife—right in front of me—that he
would never cheat on her, I knew what I was to him and I told
myself I would never go back to their place. I never did. Tonight
was the first time I've seen him in two years."

"I know I may sound like a broken record but I need to get
this straight and make a few things clear. You're free to try this—
to see where this goes? This is not a joke to you?"

"Jesus, Augusto, do I look like I'm joking to you? I just poured
my guts out to you. No one else knows about Ross. *No one.* If this

was a joke, if I just wanted sex or whatever, there's no way in hell I would've told you any of that."

"Then here's what I want you to do." Augusto took a step so his back hit the wall. He grunted softly. "I want you to kiss me."

CHAPTER TWENTY-FOUR

"I want you to kiss me."

If Alex's heart had been dammed, the floodgates opened the moment Augusto asked for that kiss. Everything inside Alex wanted to charge those beautiful honey-colored lips and devour them with the kind of savagery porn was made of, just like their first kiss had been, but this was different. Alex couldn't explain it with words, but he damn sure could with actions and this moment called for something more sincere, more passionate than a primal claiming of Augusto's mouth.

He reached up and caressed both sides of Augusto's slender neck with either hand, thumbs against the hard line of his jaw. Alex closed his eyes and leaned in slowly. He kissed the bottom lip first, mouth gently grazing Augusto's skin. The man tasted delicious—a hint of something sweet and a dash of spice. Alex licked across the seam and Augusto opened up for him.

When their tongues finally met, they twisted in the same sort of dance Alex had always craved for their bodies—massaging, licking, twirling and whirling inside each other's mouths. Alex couldn't help but moan at the feel of finally having something as pure as a sincere kiss from a man he cared about, the first man he dared to let in his heart in so long.

As he pulled back, his mouth slowly released Augusto's bottom lip, and when it slipped away, Alex fought to open his eyes again. He struggled to do that breathing thing he'd forgotten all about with their lips locked together. He inhaled deeply, then licked Augusto's sweet taste away from his bottom lip.

"I…" He couldn't even form a sentence anymore.

"Words, Alexander." A slight accent Alex hadn't heard before filled Augusto's words. Aside from that, the voice was soft and husky. "You have to use your words."

"My brain just shut down. I don't know what to say. I don't

want to ruin this."

"I think we should go for coffee," Augusto said. "If not, we're both going to get arrested for indecent exposure."

"Coffee. Right." Alex turned around and Augusto started to follow him. He spun back around, stared for a moment, then said, "Spend the night with me." When he realized what he'd blurted out, he wished he could rewind time to take it back. "I don't mean to fuck or anything. I mean…just stay the night with me. Hang out. Talk. I'll sleep on the couch if you want."

"I…" Augusto paused. "All right."

"Seriously?"

Augusto laughed. He kissed Alex's lips—a chaste kiss compared to their others—before stepping back. "I said yes."

Whatever this feeling was, Alex didn't want it to end. It was like being a kid again and waking up on Christmas Day to find everything he'd asked Santa to bring him, like being the first one picked to join the team, like being accepted to Juilliard, but somehow different. He reached down and clamped his hand around Augusto's and swore as long as he could help it, he wouldn't let go.

They headed in the direction of the nearest coffee shop. The smile had yet to fade from Alex's face, even as his mind ping-ponged around in his skull. Out of the blue, he looked over and said, "I really don't want to screw this up. If I do something stupid, it's not because I mean to. So, you tell me. If I start acting like an ass, you tell me, okay?"

"You don't have to worry about that. I promise," Augusto said.

There was something refreshing and almost calming in that promise, even if it did hold a whole lot of truthful humor. It gave Alex the confidence he needed to relax and enjoy the time he had with Augusto—whether it be short-lived or everlasting. Alex swore to himself he wouldn't harp on it, that he would do whatever it took to just enjoy Augusto's company without worrying about what might happen tomorrow.

Fingers laced together, they walked down the road to a coffee shop Alex used to frequent quite regularly, back before he lived, breathed and slept everything involved with the school. They both ordered caramel lattes and spent hours talking and laughing. Just before it was time to head home, Alex called the service to send a sedan back out to pick them up.

At Alex's apartment, his nerves started to unravel again. Everything he had was lavish, top of the line, pompous and screamed of the money he came from. He didn't want any of that to be thrown up in Augusto's face, but there wasn't a whole lot he could do about it at this point. He could only hope and pray that asking Augusto back to his place didn't backfire on him.

He unlocked the door and held it open for Augusto to enter first. Alex flipped the light switch immediately to his right. His apartment lit up in a shower of dim down lights, soft golden glow cast about every surface—from the bamboo flooring and stainless steel appliances, to the leather seating and huge flat screen. Everything in the room was custom ordered or custom made, selected by an interior designer who'd been on his father's payroll since before Alex had been born. The only thing in the room that wasn't cold and impersonal was a baby grand piano that belonged to Alex's grandfather, set off in the corner for elaborate decoration because Alex didn't have a clue how to play it.

Locking the door up tight for the evening, Alex wondered when everything would fall apart between him and Augusto again.

CHAPTER TWENTY-FIVE

The last place Augusto had visited that looked anything like this apartment was his hotel room in Paris. Though he'd only stayed there three nights before having to fly home again, he remembered the plush fabrics and perfect lighting. The pictures in Alexander's apartment were hung impersonally, not like the ones in the place he shared with Keith. Those were hung by himself, Keith and Donny. While Augusto looked around, he removed his tie and dropped it on one of the leather sofas as he slowly walked in.

Light bathed everything, glistening off things that seemed as though hadn't been used in a while. He turned to see Alexander watching him intently. At the piano he lifted the lid and tapped his finger against one key, allowed the sound to resonate within him before moving his fingers to another key. Inhaling deeply, he closed the lid and continued his small tour of the vast room.

For some reason he thought back to what Alexander had said when he asked him to stay the night.

"I don't mean to fuck or anything. I mean…just stay the night with me. Hang out. Talk. I'll sleep on the couch if you want."

He blushed and looked away. At the window, he pulled the curtain aside and stared out. They were high up. The ride in the elevator didn't seem that long. That was probably because he couldn't concentrate on anything but Alexander clutching his hand, making his heart race. Swallowing the lump in his throat, he turned and pressed his back to the cool window. "This is lovely."

Alexander seemed nervous, almost as one would look on a first date.

Augusto smiled. "Can I get something to drink?" he asked, as a way to break the intensity in the air.

"Shit. Sorry," Alex blurted, eyes widening as if he'd just now remembered to breathe. "I have bottled water. No sodas. Juice.

I can make coffee." He started toward the fridge. The room was wide open so Augusto could watch every step he took. "What would you like?"

Augusto shook his head. "I don't really like coffee that much. I take a sip in the mornings but that's about it." He extended his hand to Alexander. "Come here."

Reaching out, Alexander slowly stepped toward him again. Though there was still a lot of worry on his face, Alex's expression softened slightly. He took Augusto's hand.

Gently pulling Alexander closer, Augusto only stopped when Alexander rested into his body, pressing Augusto into the coolness of the glass. Augusto wrapped his arms around him, sliding one hand up Alex's back and caressed the tender spot at his neck. The soft touch morphed slightly into a half-handed massage while his other hand remained against Alexander's lower back.

Each breath Alexander breathed, Augusto felt against the sensitive skin of his neck and when a soft purr left Alexander's lips, a smile stretched across Augusto's face.

"I can't believe I'm actually here right now," Alexander whispered.

"Why not?" Augusto was shocked at the sound of his own voice. It was harsh, raspy to his own ears. But he couldn't hide the fact having Alexander so close affected him.

"Honestly?" Alexander raised his head. "I didn't think I could fix the first impression you had of me. I had all these great excuses for why I am the way I am, but didn't care enough to change until you made me realize how bad I am to people. Honestly, I thought I screwed up so bad I would never have a chance with you."

"You have my mom and brother to thank for this then," Augusto admitted. "I wasn't going to allow it. I'm a different kind of guy, Alexander. But we shouldn't be talking about that now. It just seems to ruin the moment."

Augusto rested his head on Alexander's shoulder. He felt Alexander's arms tighten around him, as if Alexander had only then gathered the nerve to actually hold him. Augusto embraced him completely. Then he heard a soft, "Don't let go," leave Alexander's lips.

Saying nothing, Augusto moved his head slightly, causing his lips to trace up Alexander's face. The climb went by Alexander's mouth and he stopped to drop a kiss to Alexander's nose. He twisted his head to brush his lips across Alexander's forehead. There was no way he could go the whole night without doing more than hold Alexander. But Augusto knew he couldn't be another Ross. He couldn't take advantage of that scared little boy he'd seen in Alexander's eyes from across the theatre. The one thing he knew for certain was that he would hold this man in his arms for as long as Alexander needed him to.

Shit. No! No! No!

Those were dangerous thoughts. But as hard as he fought to make them not manifest—the thought of love—each second he allowed Alexander to cling to him, the word he'd feared since Kemar's death formed another letter.

L-O…

CHAPTER TWENTY-SIX

Before even opening his eyes, Augusto felt the foreignness of the bed he lay in. It was too soft and when he stretched his free arm out it didn't hang off the side. A warm body cuddled into his chest and for a moment he panicked, wondering who he'd done the night before and why he couldn't remember. Then it all came back, washing over him like a wave on a hot day. He was with Alexander Benton, top shit at Julliard and they'd done nothing but hold each other all night until they'd fallen asleep.

He smiled and opened his eyes to find Alexander still sleeping, one hand pressed possessively against Augusto's abs. For a moment he merely lay there, enjoying the intimacy of that position, knowing it was way better than any sex they could have had. But Augusto wasn't one to sleep in and lying in bed for so long made him think of a future with Alexander, one he was still on the edge about. Reluctantly, he peeled his body from the bed, wearing nothing but his boxers. He glanced over his shoulder at Alexander's sleeping form and had to brush a finger over one of his shoulders. Augusto escaped the room before he kissed his bed buddy awake and buried himself to the hilt within him.

Instead, he made his way into the kitchen and spent a good ten minutes trying to figure out how to work the coffeemaker. It resembled a contraption that should've been in a spaceship, *not* in a kitchen. "What in the hell? This isn't even in…" He stopped and pressed a button. The machine beeped, a green light came on and he watched the pot. Finally, a drop of coffee landed in it and he sighed. "Well, that didn't take a bloody long time at all."

He didn't want to just sit around watching it brew so he wandered around the apartment to find the bathroom and after quickly using it, he made his way back to the living room. The piano in the corner called to him. It'd been a while since he'd really played aside from a few taps of the keys.

Sliding his hand over the cover, he tried remembering the

last time he played before an audience. He was about seventeen and his mother had asked him as a favor to play for her church until they could find a new pianist. Augusto sat astride the bench and lifted the lid. He started playing *Dum Da Dum* by Shawn Desmond. He rested one elbow against the piano with his fingers shoved through his hair. After taking a breath, he played softly with his eyes closed.

§§§

A sound Alex hadn't heard since his grandfather had been alive filled the air with melodic serenity. It was a good way to wake up after the night he'd spent with a man who had been filling every corner of his dreams for some time now. He ran his hand down the spot where he just knew Augusto's muscled abs would still be.

They weren't there.

Augusto was gone!

What the hell? The thought made him bolt straight up in the bed.

It took a minute for his panic to settle and the fog of his sleepy brain to clear, when it finally did, he untwisted himself from the bed linens then padded into the other room. He found Augusto's tan, lithe body perched on the wooden bench, fingers gracefully floating over the keys. It was incredibly spellbinding to watch and Alex couldn't make himself look away. In fact, to be very honest, he found himself rather aroused by the beauty in what he saw.

The music died down and Alex started in with a slow clap, the smile on his face so wide he could feel his cheeks pushing up against his eyes. Augusto swung around, now straddling the bench. Alex wanted to be the body beneath him so badly.

"Beautiful," Alex said, dropping his hands to his sides as he pushed up from the doorframe. He started across the room toward Augusto because he couldn't make himself stay away.

"Thanks." Augusto reached a hand up for him. "My brother is better. I'm the guitar player in the family. Donny is the pianist and Mammie is the voice. How did you sleep?"

"Better than I've slept in…forever." Alex let Augusto guide him down to the bench. They both straddled it, facing each other. It took everything Alex had in him not to lean in for another kiss.

But it seemed Augusto wasn't fighting that emotion. With the sweet smell of freshly brewed coffee swirling about them, Augusto cradled his face gently and leaned in like a school boy would for his first kiss. For a moment nothing happened; Augusto merely hovered his lips inches from Alex's. Then after a breath, he kissed Alex softly, molding their lips together then using his tongue to ask entry into the hot depths of Alex's mouth.

As their lips caressed and their tongues twisted and turned, Alex let go of himself. He gave in to everything he'd desired from Augusto. With his eyes closed, he pictured Augusto towering over him, playing his body just as he'd so elegantly played the piano. The music they made together just as sensual and harmonious.

Alex felt his shaft begin to pulse, his cock growing harder. It was all for Augusto. The bliss he imagined on Augusto's face as the came together spurred his erection. God, help him. He needed to make love to Augusto's beautiful, heavenly body right now.

When he realized the utter lust he felt, he broke the kiss and tried to clear his head. This was supposed to be about more than sex. Way more than what he had with Kenny.

Shit! Kenny!

Alex cleared his throat and tried swallowing down the knot. He licked his kiss swollen lips, looked Augusto in the eyes and said, "I have a confession to make."

"A confession?" Augusto released Alex and eased back on the seat. "Okay?"

"Before you came along, I was seeing someone." Alex paused, watching as Augusto's expression changed. Clearly, he was trying to remain stoic and listen, but the darkening in his eyes betrayed him. Alex continued. "I haven't had sex with him since before that night at Santo's, the night you…"

"The night I what?"

"Made me realize what an asshole I am. He came over to check on me but I made him leave. I didn't want him."

"I'm such a moron." Augusto rose. "While you were asking me to kiss you and all that, you were with someone else. I don't want to be anyone's second choice."

"Will you please just stop for a minute," Alex pleaded as he grabbed Augusto's wrist. "Listen to me. You're not my second choice."

"Did you and this other guy break-up?"

"There's nothing to break up. We're not together. Neither one of us is in love with the other. I think we were just something to pass the time." Alex sighed. "I wanted to be honest with you. You're the only person I want, and not just sexually. It's…it's deeper than that. Can't you see that now?"

"Alexander, you were sleeping with someone—a human being with feelings. How can you say it was just to pass the time?"

"Will you sit down and listen to me? I'll tell you everything."

"I'm not sure I want to hear anymore." Augusto walked to the window. "I mean—you sleep with this guy, find someone else and don't even tell him you're through. Is that what you're going to do to me?"

"No. It's not." Alex sat down on the couch, elbows pressed to his knees, hands holding up his suddenly heavy head. "Kenny and I talked right after I met you, after you kissed me. I asked him if he loved me and he said no. I was relieved because I didn't love him either. I told him that. We always had this sort of arrangement. Neither of us really wanted casual sex, but we both had needs and we were friends, so it kind of just happened. We both went into it knowing things would end if we met someone. I want you to be the someone who sends me down to Kenny's place to tell him we're not going to fuck anymore."

Alex raised his head and looked up at Augusto. His eyes burned. He could swear he felt the brewing of tears, his throat tightening, because he feared this would be what made Augusto walk away for good.

In a quiet, broken and quivering voice, Alex said, "I want you to be the one I truly fall in love with."

Chapter Twenty-seven

"What am I supposed to do with all of this?"

It felt like the end of the world.

V…E…

The word is complete—L-O-V-E

Jealousy surged through Augusto again. Alexander brought out all these things in him. He really wasn't proud of most of them. He was the *other* man, something he never wanted to be. Pressing a palm to the cool glass, he hung his head forward, feeling anger, pity and confusion race through him as if it would never stop. With his free hand he braced himself up, for if he let go, Augusto knew for sure he'd crumble to the floor.

"You know what's strange?" He spoke without looking away from the abyss he was staring into. "I thought maybe I could be your man. I wanted to be so bad, especially when I held you in my arms on that bed. All I wanted to do was to crawl in beside you every night and stay there, but Alexander we haven't even decided to date yet and already you've hurt me more than anyone else has. I don't know what to do about that."

"Augusto, you have to give me a chance. These are things that happened before you came into the picture. I told you because I want to be completely honest. Doesn't that count for something?"

"But he's still here!" Augusto banged his closed fist into the window sill. "He's still here and most importantly…" He walked to where Alexander sat and jabbed a finger against his chest and the side of Alexander's head. "Most importantly, he's here and here. I don't just want to fuck you, Alexander. I want to hold you in my arms and feel our bodies melding into one. I want to make love to you until you know the difference but I can't. I don't want to be a rebound and I don't want you running to him if we have arguments. I like being alone with my men. I don't play well with others—Do you get it? I don't share!"

Alex stood straight up from the couch. He was nose to nose with Augusto when he slammed his own hand over his heart and yelled, "You are in here. The only fucking person who has been in two years!"

"But the day before…when I almost kissed you, he touched you. Didn't he?" Augusto backed up then. He could feel a fight coming and it was the last thing he wanted to do. "I don't want to fight with you…" He turned for the door.

"Augusto," Alex all but growled.

The sound made Augusto whip his head back. He was prepared to launch into a verbal attack but before he could process what was happening, a mouth clamped over his and he was being forcibly walked backward.

His spine hit the door hard enough to push an *umf* sound into the kiss, but neither one of them relented. Suddenly, he felt Alex's tongue spear straight into his mouth, fighting to devour it. Hands flew at each other—Augusto trying to shove Alex away, Alex trying to hold on tighter. The kiss broke with a gasp and a wide-eyed stare. Neither man moved for a moment.

All that passed between them was air and the soft pants of lungs sucking in air. Still they stood there, Augusto with his head turned away from Alexander, his lungs burning sweetly from the kiss. His lips tingled wonderfully and his fingers curled into fists by his sides. His body battled with his mind and heart. His mind lost horribly. Slowly, he lifted his right hand and placed it against Alexander's right shoulder. The flesh burned him, causing a soft hiss to escape his lips. With his eyes closed, he stepped into Alex's embrace, gripped his left shoulder and found his mouth again. This time there was no fighting, no pretense. This time, he hungered and no amount of kissing, of tasting Alex's mouth seemed to be quelling the blaze roaring within him. Shoving a hand down the front of Alex's boxers, Augusto massaged, feeling Alex's dick react to him and harden. He wrenched his mouth back and exhaled like blowing smoke from a cigarette.

"Holy fuck…" Alex rasped, eyelids fluttering as Augusto gripped his cock. "What are…are… Ah, shit."

Augusto yanked his hand back at the outburst. "Do you want me to stop, Alex?"

"Hell no," Alex breathed raggedly, pulling Augusto's hand back. "Don't ever stop."

"Is that your way of asking nicely?" Augusto backed away in the direction of the bedroom. "I need you to dance for me now. Shake your ass a little."

"I'm not supposed to be dancing, but I think I can manage for you."

Alex started in a slow walk, fingers tucked in the waistband of his boxers. Something almost lewd passed through his eyes. He pulled the fabric down until his rock hard cock sprang free. Alex lifted up on the balls of his feet and spun around. When he stopped, his bare ass was in the air, aimed at Augusto and begging to be taken.

Augusto merely stepped forward and traced a finger over Alexander's skin. He memorized the soft hairs against it, the roundness of those perfectly dimpled cheeks, even the heat that soothed his hand. Every pass of his hands pushed his desires further, higher, until he had Alexander's ass right in his groin. A soft growl eased from his body and his lips found Alex's ear.

"Push back harder," Augusto demanded. "I want you to feel this."

On his command, Alex bowed at the waist, spreading his cheeks wider. His rosette became a target, and he rolled his hips, grinding his ass against Augusto's groin, adding enough pressure to push the fabric of Augusto's boxers along his shaft.

"It's all yours," Alex breathed. "All you have to do is take it." And he rolled his hips again.

"Shit," Augusto swore. "You have to show me where the condoms are."

Alex stood, rolling his ass over Augusto's crotch again. He

spun around and grabbed Augusto's wrist to pull him further into the bedroom where they'd slept the night before.

"Look in the top drawer of the nightstand," Alex said, sitting on the edge of the bed. He had one leg hanging off the side and the other hiked up to the mattress, hard cock jutting out from between his thighs. He kept his stare trained on Augusto as he fondled himself.

"You are trying to drive me crazy," Augusto whispered, reaching over for the drawer without looking. He wasn't familiar with the room but he felt around until he got what he wanted along with lube. He stood away from Alexander, watching him touch himself and feeling his own cock jump with excitement. Still he was patient. He slowly stripped for Alexander, sheathed his cock into a condom and lubed it. Then and only then did he walk over to the bed and sit on it. He scooted until his back hit the headboard and spread his legs.

"Climb, on Alex…Let's see how well you ride."

"For you, anything."

Alex seductively rolled onto his knees. He kissed Augusto's thigh, then his navel and his nipple. He straddled Augusto's legs as he aimed his channel over the tip of Augusto's cock. Reaching behind, he rolled his hand over Augusto's sac before encircling his shaft.

"Tell me you want this, Augusto," Alex said, but it wasn't the kind of sexy bed talk Augusto expected. It seemed more like Alex needed reassurance.

"I want…" Augusto's voice broke. He cleared his throat, pressed his back harder to the headboard and licked his lips. "I want you to take my cock as deep as you can take it."

Closing his eyes, Alex exhaled and lowered his body slowly, easing Augusto's cock through his tightened ring of muscle.

A sigh of satisfaction filled the air as Augusto tried desperately not to take control of the situation. It was hard but he eased his bum up and pressed his hands beneath him then sat again. He slid within Alexander, inch by glorious inch and all he could do was give in to the engulfing fire. His lover held him tight and slick before sliding off only to impale himself again. Augusto watched him, seeing the sheer pleasure in his face. Then Alexander clamped around him and pulled up.

"Alex…" he rasped.

CHAPTER TWENTY-EIGHT

Each time Alex slid down over Augusto's shaft, he moaned a little louder. A feeling of euphoria, of absolute bliss washed over him. He'd never experienced anything like this with anyone else, not even Ross. This wasn't just sex. It was spiritual.

With his head thrown back and his eyes closed, he rode his beautiful lover. His leg muscles curled and flexed with every thrust. He lifted himself up slowly, then slammed back down, burying Augusto's cock deep inside him. In and out. In and out, giving a slight roll of the hips each time, and every time he came back down, he could feel himself reaching the edge of release.

Augusto's fingers locked around his, lacing them together as their palms met in a kiss. The feel of that sudden strong grip made Alex raise his head and open his eyes. He looked down and what he saw was a vision of beauty, pure and unadulterated, in the throes of true passion.

His lover bit down on his plump bottom lip hard enough to turn his tan skin a soft shade of honey. Augusto's eyes were open, watching every move Alex made, his big brown stare weighted with the kind of lust that made Alex want to devour him. Beyond the carnal hunger though, there was something warm and genuine about the way Augusto watched him, something…loving.

"Oh, God," Alex rasped, clenching his eyes shut again.

He rose and slid back down, slower this time because he wanted to prolong the pleasure. But it didn't matter how slow he went, because every time Augusto's wonderfully thick shaft pushed deep into him, filled his channel and ever so gently rubbed across Alex's sweet spot, the will to hang on broke away.

"I'm about to come," he breathed.

His stamina was wearing thin way too fast and he silently cursed himself for not holding on longer, but the moment Augusto commanded Alex to "come for him," he lost all control.

His sac tightened against his body. His shaft began to pulse. Pearly ropes of pure bliss erupted from the head of his cock, and it took everything Alex had not to collapse on top of Augusto's body.

Now Augusto started to roll his hips—a spicy little dance that kept his cock pumping in and out of Alex with a nicely sensual rhythm. He tightened his fingers around Alex's hand, holding Alex right where Augusto so obviously wanted him. Alex didn't mind, even if he wanted to curl around Augusto's body and pass out for a few hours. The view was still utterly perfect—the way sweat clung to Augusto's toned, muscled, rippled chest, the way Augusto bit down on his lip and grunted ever so slightly when he buried himself inside Alex's body, the way the edges of his lips pushed into faint dimples when he eased back out. The sight mesmerized Alex.

"You're beautiful," Alex breathed airily, not really meaning for those words to find life at all.

The traces of a smile graced Augusto's lips and his fingers tightened with Alex's for a moment longer then loosened. His arm went around Alex's back and flipped him to the bed without them separating. Then Augusto was over him, looking down at him while hiking Alex's legs up and wide. He released the other hand, braced both palms on Alex's chest and rode him long and hard.

"I want to see the look in your eyes as you come," Augusto whispered. "I want you to look straight at me."

"That's so fucking hot," Alex rasped in return, verbal filter failing miserably. He couldn't help it though. Augusto turned him into an open book.

With one foot hooked on the headboard and the heel of his other pressed to the mattress, Alex was wide open for his lover, able to move enough to add a little heat to their romance. As Augusto slammed down, Alex bucked his torso. They met in a hot kiss of sweaty bodies, ass to groin. Alex felt a heated flutter ripple through him. Augusto was about to make him come again.

Augusto reached for one of Alex's nipples, pinching and twisting as he rolled his hips forward. He sank deep inside Alex. He didn't stop. It was as if Augusto needed him to come as badly as Alex wanted to.

Arching his back, Alex clenched his jaw and let the second wave of heated pleasure tear through him. This time it was ten times more intense. The feeling was more than just release and relief, it was thrill of being conquered and controlled by someone equally as dominant as he'd always been.

"Shit!" Alex growled as heat burst from the head of his cock. The one word faded into a high-pitched whimper as his entire body began to tingle. He had one of those *do not touch me* moments some men got after shooting their load, but the more Augusto did touch him, the more that feeling was driven away.

Augusto used soft caresses to soothe him. He trailed a finger down Alex's chest barely skimming the skin as he leaned in to take Alex's lips in a gentle kiss that wasn't any less fiery than the rough ones they'd shared before.

Curling his fingers in Augusto's hair, Alex gave in to the passion of the kiss. He let it embrace him and caress his soul as he stroked his thumbs behind his lover's ears. Augusto rolled his hips slower now, so slowly every time he pulled back, the veiny surface of his shaft tickled every nerve in Alex's body.

Reluctantly, Alex pulled back from the kiss. He licked his swollen lips and whispered, "Come for me, baby. It's my turn to watch."

Chapter Twenty-nine

Augusto eased his hips back, slid from Alexander and pulled him into his arms. Though he hadn't orgasmed, he felt more fulfilled than he had in a very long time. He wanted to explode too but he saw how drained Alexander was and couldn't possibly make him go another round. Smiling, he knew there would be another time. He turned his lips to drop featherlight kisses to Alexander's forehead, while rubbing one hand up and down his back. It was a strange thing to be this intimate with someone and kissing was the closest any two people could ever be. He felt a draw to Alex, leaving him weak and trembling against his lover. The dark thoughts of second guessing started pushing their heads to the surface though. Augusto groaned and pressed his eyes shut tight as if that would stop them. The action did for a moment before the sinking feeling returned and he shifted slightly.

"What does this mean now?" he questioned out loud before he could stop himself. "Does this mean we're friends with benefits or are we only seeing each other?"

"I told you, I *only* want to see you. More so now than I did before."

"Sometimes everything seems clear when you're on the conquest, then when you finally get what you want, it doesn't look so good afterward."

Alex tilted his head to the side, staring up at Augusto. "Do you think that's what happened here?"

"I don't know. I definitely don't want to jump to any conclusions. That's why I'm asking."

"I guess it'll take time to prove to you just how genuine I am."

Augusto chuckled. "My mom has this saying, *The road to Rome is paved with the best intentions.'* We'll go slow and see where things lead us. I want it to lead to something serious but no pressure.

Anyway, what are your plans for the rest of the day?"

"Good intentions…with you." Alex gave him a playful grin.

"I see the way you look at me, *Cariño*." He said the endearment before he could stop himself. "There are no good intentions there." Augusto laughed softly while turning his head to kiss Alex's forehead again.

"Actually, there really are." Alex splayed his hand at the small of Augusto's back. "Only the best for you. In fact, I think I need to make a phone call to someone. He needs to know we won't be seeing each other anymore."

Augusto said nothing for a moment. He was trying to rein in the feelings pulsing through him so he didn't overreact. Finally, he nodded. "I should head home soon anyway. I need a change of clothes, gotta pay a few bills after picking up my paycheck. The trains don't run that well on the weekends."

"I was hoping to hang out with you today." Alex pouted. "Stay. I'll get the car service to take you back later. Just…stay with me today. Please?"

The soft breath on Alex's pleading caused Augusto to close his eyes and swallow a lump that had suddenly formed in his throat. He really needed to work out how he was going to pay for his third semester. The first two were covered by a scholarship Luther had at the club but after that he'd be pretty much on his own. Taking a breath, he opened his eyes and looked down into Alex's face. His resolve weakened and he bowed his head to kiss the pink pout of Alex's lips.

"All right. But I can't stay too late. Keith will put out a missing persons on me."

"You're free to leave whenever you need but, baby, I can't promise I won't protest."

Augusto chuckled. "Come on. I should feed you."

"Mmm…Feed me." Alex laughed. "Actually, why don't I call for takeout and while we're waiting, we can both get showered? I know a great Thai place."

"Why do I get the feeling the feeding you were thinking of and the one I was thinking of are different?" He grinned. "I can't eat Thai. I'd be useless for the rest of the day. I would suggest some Spanish food but I'm sure the only thing keeping you from tying me to this bed is if I promise not to leave it?"

"Tied to the bed, eh? I have to tell you, seeing you bound onstage at Santo's turned me on so damn bad." It was Alex's turn to roll their bodies, his turn to be on top again. He kissed the middle of Augusto's sternum. "I got so hard watching you dance," he purred as his kisses travelled lower. He pulled the condom from Augusto's shaft. "I imagined us like that. Fucking. Dancing. I lusted for you like I never did with anyone else." And with those last words, he lowered his lips and sheathed Augusto's cock with his mouth.

He didn't expect that. Augusto thought for sure Alex was tired and just needed rest. At Alex's confession he got it—him grinding with the other dancer meant Alex was seeing Augusto in his head. That realization hardened him and with his lover's mouth lathering his dick with saliva, he was too weak to do much of anything but lie there. Holding the back of Alex's neck, he rolled his hips upward slowly, pushing the head of his cock to the back of Alex's throat.

"So…damn…good…"

CHAPTER THIRTY

As crazy as it seemed, when Sunday morning came along and Alex had to say good-bye to Augusto, his heart felt heavier than it had in a while. He didn't want Augusto to leave, not right now, not any time soon, and who knew, maybe not ever. The last two nights had been the most amazing he'd had in far too long. But Alex had something important to do, something he needed to do alone, something that had to be done before he could be in a real relationship with the man he'd been falling so hard for and he wouldn't waste another second taking that final leap into a life of being committed to someone else.

"Kenny?" Alex said into the phone after he heard a groggy voice say a gravelly hello. "It's Alex. I need to talk to you. Can you come up?"

"I have to get dressed."

There was another groan, but it didn't come from Alex, and it damn sure wasn't soft and sweet enough to come from Carolynne. Sounded like Kenny had another man in his bed, and if he did, that just made this whole situation much easier to deal with.

"Take your time," Alex said. "I'll be here alone all day." Unfortunately.

He waited for Kenny to grumble in agreement, and when his soon to be ex-lover did, Alex said a swift good-bye then laid his phone down on the kitchen counter.

This was absolutely the right thing to do. No doubt about it. Augusto deserved his loyalty. Augusto deserved a faithful man, and that's exactly what Alex wanted to be to him, but that didn't change the fact Alex had to hurt someone he cared about in the process, which made Alex feel about as low as he had the night Augusto had told him just how truly horrible he was.

As the big break-up speech wound around in his head, playing on infinite loop, Alex stared out the window and down at all the rich passersby climbing into sedans and walking their designer dogs or strutting hand in hand with someone they might or might not love. That was the life Alex had grown accustomed to, a life that didn't leave a lot of room for genuinely healthy relationships.

For a moment he thought about everything Augusto had told him, about how the beautiful Latino dancer didn't want to be just another screw, how Augusto didn't do casual sex and he was the kind of man who wanted love, who wanted a committed relationship. Alex was ninety-nine-point-nine percent certain he could give Augusto that sort of undying, unconditional love, but what if he messed up? What if this turned out to be another Ross situation where Alex fell head over heels for someone, and that special someone turned around and destroyed him?

No, you can't think like that. Augusto isn't Ross.

The doorbell ringing jerked him away from those thoughts and none too soon. Alex was on the verge of convincing himself that entering into any kind of relationship would be a mistake because he was far too broken to trust that anyone could love him. He padded across the room and opened the door, only to find Kenny standing there in nothing but a pair of faded jeans, his hair tousled and hickeys on his chest.

"Wow. Looks like you had a wild night," Alex said, turning away from the open door so Kenny could follow him in.

"I can explain."

"You don't have to, Kenneth. My weekend was just as fun-filled as yours obviously was."

"You're not mad?"

Smirking, Alex turned back around to face his former booty call. The smile on Alex's face widened. The fear in Kenneth's eyes deepened. "No, I'm not mad at all. In fact, that's what I wanted to talk to you about."

Alex headed around the kitchen island, back to the counter where the coffeemaker waited patiently to brew up a pot of the good stuff. Kenneth sat down on one of the barstools, watching as Alex moved about the open room.

"This thing we've been doing," Alex said. "We can't do it anymore. I've met someone, and I—"

"I met someone too!"

"—I think I'm in love with him."

"Oh." Kenneth scrubbed his hands up and down his jeans. He couldn't seem to make eye contact anymore. "Love. That's... big. Doesn't just happen overnight. How long you been seeing him?"

"I've been *wanting* to see him since freshman auditions. We kissed a few times, but they were angry kisses. He hated me. I despised him for it, but at the same time, I lusted over him. We finally made love this weekend." Alex lowered his head. Though he'd never considered what he'd done with Augusto cheating, now, with Kenneth staring right through him, he sort of did.

When Alex looked back up to continue his speech, he found Kenneth still staring. Alex cleared his throat and continued. "The point is I want to be in a relationship with him. I only want to be with him. That means I can't see you anymore. Okay?"

"Alex, it's fine. I promise. Like I said, I met someone too. I don't know if it's love yet, but I like him. He's a good guy, strong, but caring. He makes me laugh."

"That's perfect, Kenneth."

Kenny stood from the bench and headed around the island. He wrapped his hand around Alex's wrist and pulled Alex into a tight hug. There wasn't anything sexual about the way they held each other, it was the kind of embrace long-lasting friendships were made of, the kind that embedded into one's memory and stayed there a lifetime. Parting wasn't sweet sorrow for either of them, because what they'd had served its purpose, and just as they'd promised to each other, when they met new men and formed new relationships, they would move on from what they had and remain friends.

"I should go back to my apartment," Kenneth whispered as

he released Alex from his hold.

"Yeah, I need to call Augusto. I told him I would as soon as I finished speaking with you."

Kenny nodded. "I really wish you guys the best of luck."

"You too, Kenneth. I hope you always have happiness."

"So far,"—Kenny grinned—"it's been incredible."

Alex laughed softly. "Same here."

Watching Kenneth leave, Alex kept the smile on his face and waited for the door to close behind him. Now that the big break-up was done and he knew he still had a friend in Kenneth, he felt like he could breathe a lot easier. He could be a better man to Augusto, the kind of man who could vow undying devotion to someone else and mean every word of it.

He grabbed his phone from the counter and carried it over to the couch. He sank down amongst the fluffy pillows, still smelling Augusto's cologne in their fibers. With unwavering zeal and an unfading smile on his face, he punched in Augusto's number then waited and waited as it rang. Eventually the voicemail answered, but that didn't deter Alex's happiness.

"I did it," he said, and even he could hear the wide smile in his own voice. "I broke it off with Kenny and it went really well. He already had someone new and I…It doesn't matter. It's over between me and Kenny, and Augusto, I only want you. Now. Tomorrow. Ten thousand tomorrows from now. I. Want. You."

CHAPTER THIRTY-ONE

Augusto meant to use his Sunday to run some errands but wound up going to work. Chet was sick and since Augusto choreographed the routines for Chet's guys, they called him to fill in. By the time the night drew to a close, he was exhausted to the point of wanting to pass out. Alone in the dance room, he flipped off the light and was closing the door when he heard Luther calling his name.

He turned and waved, closing the door before heading down the hall to walk beside his mentor and one time father-in-law. "How did you like tonight?" Augusto questioned.

"It was good—very good. The crowd seemed to like the new routines. But that wasn't what I wanted to talk to you about. You got a minute?"

"Luther I…"

"Gus, please. This is important."

Augusto stared at him for a brief instant then nodded.

"I'm getting old."

"Luther?"

"Let me finish. This place was supposed to be Kemar's. He's all the family I had left in the world and after the cancer took him, I had no one. But you didn't leave me. You stayed here and since you're like a son to me I—well, I had my will changed during the week and I didn't want it to be a surprise for you."

"Are you sick? What can I do?"

Luther smiled softly. "No, son. I'm not sick. But with my age, one never knows. I always like to be prepared."

"Damn it, Luther."

"Damn me if you want. But it won't change the fact this place will be yours after I'm gone. I don't trust anyone else to have it because I know you will handle it with care."

"Don't talk like that, Luther. You're not going anywhere."

"Are we looking at the same face I see every time I look in the mirror? I know what you're trying to say and I appreciate it. Just know I'd rather burn this joint to the ground than see some money hungry loser take it over. You know the value of this place. You know how important dance and music—real music—is to me and Kemar. No one else understands."

"But I'm going to have school and a career.'"

"I'm not planning on dying any day soon. I'll keep running the place until I either get too old or you are ready to take over or the big bell tolls for me. It's just something I wanted to do now before it's too late."

"And what if I told you I'm seeing someone—someone I'm serious about?"

"I'd say good for you. About damn time."

"It doesn't make you mad?"

"Augusto, we had this conversation. Now, go home. I know you weren't expecting to work tonight and I'm sorry. You should rest up for classes tomorrow."

Augusto nodded and after a pat on the shoulder, he made his way out the door. Suddenly, he stopped, his mind went blank for a brief second before he darted into the room again. Stopping before Luther, he took a breath before hugging the old man tightly. *"Gracias por todos."*

"Oh, you're welcome, son."

"Want me to stick around and walk you to your car?" Augusto questioned, stepping back when Luther grunted from the force of his arms around him.

"No. Mark is still here. He will see to it I get home safely. You go. I still have some receipts I have to go through and print."

Normally, Augusto would stick his music in the moment he was outside but the cool air washing over his skin didn't allow that. He wanted to enjoy the night. But Luther's words sent a dark cloud over him. Sure he would love to run Santo's at some point but the thought that Luther had to die for him to do so broke his heart. Shoving his hands into his pockets, he pulled out his phone to check his messages and saw he had three new voicemails.

The first was from Keith. The second was from some bank trying to give him a credit card.

Like I need another one of those.

And the third was from the one voice Augusto wanted to hear so badly. It was Alexander with the best news a guy could get. He was the one—the only. His heart did a little flip so he jumped, clicked his heels and shoved his hands back into his pockets. It was a stupid thing but he just couldn't help himself. He whistled *Dum Da Dum* and hurried into the subway. Walking home was out of the question—he was just too tired.

At home he checked in on his roommate to find Keith fast asleep, naked on his bed. Shaking his head, Augusto pulled the sheets up to Keith's hips and closed the door quietly behind him. Replaying Alexander's message over in his head, he grabbed a bottle of juice from the fridge, made his way to his bed and called Alex.

"I've been waiting to hear your voice all day," Alex said instead of giving him a standard hello. "You got my message, I assume."

Augusto rolled to his back, crossed his ankles and slipped his free hand behind his head. "I did. I'm sorry it's so late but I had to fill in for the lead dancer on my last day off."

"Better late than never, baby."

"How are you taking the break-up? Are you all right?"

"I'm good, actually. He came over covered in hickeys and his hair was a mess. Apparently, he met someone too." Alex paused. "We wished each other the best. It wasn't bad at all."

"That's good. I hated feeling as if I caused another guy pain in any way. It sucks to be dumped for someone else."

"Nothing to worry about there. No harm done." Alex paused again. Augusto heard what he swore sounded like the rustling of bed linens. It sounded like Alex was climbing out of bed. Alex said, "Tomorrow night, why don't you stay in town with me? It's easier than trying to go all the way home after school."

"Tomorrow night I work," Augusto told him. "I get Tuesday off so if you want I can stay with you then."

"Mmm…" Alex whined. "I have to wait until Tuesday to see you again?"

"I'm in classes all day Monday. We can steal some time between classes so we can …er …talk."

"Won't be there tomorrow. I have a doctor's appointment. They're supposed to tell me if I'll ever dance again."

Augusto sat up on the bed at those words and took a breath. "You'll let me know how that goes? I can call in sick and come with you."

"I'll be fine. Carolynne is supposed to go. Besides, if they say I can't dance anymore, I don't want you to see me turn into a blubbering idiot."

Augusto chuckled softly. "What do these doctors know anyways? They told my mom she could never have kids. Imagine her surprise when I came into the world kicking and screaming."

Alex laughed. "Oh, I know I'll be fine. It was just a broken toe. I think,"—the line went quiet and Augusto had to double check to make sure the call hadn't been dropped—"I think I'm waiting for karma to kick my ass, you know?"

"Why do you say that? For a few broken hearts you left along the way? Karma has other things to do. Just don't beat yourself up about all that now."

"I don't know, Augusto. I'm realizing what a piece of shit I've always been. That's not an easy thing to learn about yourself, baby."

"That's true. But you have to learn to forgive yourself…you want to go away with me the following weekend?"

"Will you let me pay your way?"

Augusto rolled his eyes and flopped to the bed. "Here's my compromise. You can pay for the rental car to get up there. We have a place to stay, all we need is a ride and food."

"Then yes, I will go with you."

"Are you sure?"

"Absolutely. I look forward to it."

"Good. Now get some sleep," Augusto told him. "I would have enjoyed tucking you in."

"I would've enjoyed sleeping beside you," Alex admitted. "Maybe we can explore a change of residence for you soon. No pressure. Just a thought."

Augusto made no reply to that. He wasn't about to leave Keith with the whole rent. They promised to stick it out until school was over. He grunted. "Good night, Alex."

"Good night, gorgeous."

CHAPTER THIRTY-TWO

The week dragged on and on, passing by slower than it ever had before. Alex couldn't wait to get away with Augusto. They'd even spent time away from each other to make the days they would have together so much sweeter, and the time apart turned Alex into an obsessive junky dying to get his next fix.

His bags had been packed since Wednesday, and his driver was told to be prompt at nine in the morning Friday or the wrath he would have to face would be catastrophic. Alex'd meant every word too. And when the sedan pulled in front of his apartment that morning, Alex felt like he could finally breathe again.

The driver loaded his suitcase into the trunk. Alex climbed into the backseat, cradling a bouquet of twelve red roses against his chest. They smelled divine and he couldn't wait to see the smile on Augusto's beautiful face when he finally arrived.

It took more than forty-five minutes for them to finally arrive in Augusto's neighborhood. The place didn't look safe at all—rundown, dirty, thugs hanging out on the corners, whores walking the streets. It was typical of many New York neighborhoods that all kinds of people lived in, but Augusto wasn't just *any* kind of person. He was special and so very precious. He was so much better than that place, worth so much more.

Yeah, Alex would totally broach the subject of making Augusto his roommate again, on a much more serious level this time. He didn't like the looks of this neighborhood one bit.

"Would you like to get him or would you like to wait in the car?" the driver asked.

Neither option felt safe.

Alex opened his mouth to answer when he saw Augusto descend a flight of steps. He let out a sigh of relief—both to finally see his man again and to not be left alone in the car. The driver immediately hopped out and took Augusto's bag, opening the back door so Alex's boyfriend could climb inside.

"Hey, gorgeous," he said, leaning over to meet Augusto in a chaste kiss. "Flowers. For you."

One of Augusto's brows shot up as he took the bouquet and accepted the kiss. "You brought me flowers?"

"Yeah." Alex shrugged. The flowers were a big deal to him. They meant something, something huge since he didn't go out of his way to buy people flowers, but... "Just a small token of my"—*don't say love, not yet, you'll kill the moment*—"gratitude."

"They're beautiful," Augusto whispered, leaning in for a more meaningful kiss just as the door closed behind him. "Thank you."

"Anything for you."

Closing his eyes, Alex leaned in to steal another taste of the wonderfully sensual lips he'd grown quite addicted to. He placed his hand on Augusto's hip, holding him in place as their tongues twisted in a dance. It was just as delicious as every other time Augusto had kissed him, maybe even made sweeter by the time they'd spent apart.

The car pulling forward broke the kiss and Alex gave him a dazed smile. He wanted so badly to declare his love for Augusto, but it had to wait. The timing had to be right. In the back of a car, pulling out of a seedy part of town just didn't have the air of romance Alex wanted when he finally got the balls to utter those three little words.

No. No, it most definitely had to wait.

Alex bit back the words, cleared his throat and gave Augusto a tight smile. "I've missed you so much this week," he said, reaching up to push a long curly tendril of black hair from Augusto's handsome face, tucking it softly behind Augusto's ear.

"This whole staying apart thing was your idea." Augusto smiled at Alex as he slid a hand over his abs. "I was perfectly happy to come over in the middle of the night, pretend to be your secret lover and have my way with your very delectable, very tight body with a blindfold and some molten chocolate. But..."

He stopped speaking to drag the hand upward and pinch one of Alex's nipples through his shirt. "You had a better idea."

"Keep that up"—Alex purred, reaching to move Augusto's hand southward—"and the driver will be taking the very, very scenic route to the rental place."

He chuckled and squeezed Alex's cock. "I was thinking more along the lines of a little fun in the rental car once we get it. Come on, Alex. You were thinking it too."

"Frankly, my dear, I've been thinking of having you anywhere I can get you." He arched into Augusto's hand, pumping his hardening cock against the firmness of his lover's grip. "We could...right now...I could raise the partition and you could make me come. Right here. With someone on the other side of a very thin wall, someone who might hear us if I accidentally get too loud."

Augusto laughed. "I was going to ask you on what planet you'd think he wouldn't know what we were doing back here." But even as he said these words, he used a couple of fingers to undo the button on Alex's jeans. He licked at Alex's neck, nipping the flesh. "You may want to get that partition up." He snaked his hand into Alex's pants and pressed his hot palm to the hardened muscle there and squeezed.

Blindly reaching over, Alex fumbled the switches on the door beside him. The locks clicked. The window went up and down. He arched against Augusto's palm, moaning as his man applied a beautiful amount of pressure to his groin. Alex moaned louder and the door locks clicked again. He forgot all about the partition and his hand went straight to Augusto's hair, twining his fingers in all those pitch black silken locks.

"I'll handle the partition, Mr. Benton," the driver said, watching through the rearview mirror.

"Mhm..." Alex groaned as Augusto freed his cock.

Finally. Privacy.

A soft sound emanated from Augusto's body, a low rattling. Alex pulled back to see Augusto was laughing. "You're pulling away? Come on, baby." Augusto chuckled. "Focus."

"You have your hand on my cock and you want me to focus? I'm doing good just breathing, honey."

Augusto smiled even as he stroked Alex with a hard fist. "Let's see how loud you can get." He smirked, tightening his fingers. "Let…me…hear…you…scream."

The stroking became faster, more fervent and almost feverish. Alex resisted. The game they were playing was just too damn fun and the more he held out, the harder Augusto worked to get him off. It didn't take too long though. That soft palm riding up and down his shaft, the thumb tickling his slit, the nerve endings buzzing to life—it all did him in and within minutes, the growl that had been brewing in his chest turned into a full-fledged scream. The orgasm he'd been holding onto culminated in a pearly explosion that sprayed thick ropes of cum across the back of the leather seat.

Alex sunk down in his seat, breathing hard through clenched teeth, eyes rolling back in his head. "Fuck."

The profanity was barely out of his mouth before Augusto's lips covered his. He released Alex's cock after a few last pumps before stroking Alex's inner thighs.

CHAPTER THIRTY-THREE

The moment the car stopped Alexander rushed from it to pee, making Augusto laugh. Augusto took the suitcase from the trunk of their rental car and placed it on the porch of the cabin, before returning for the other one. Once he had all the bags out of the car including the half empty bags of mixed nuts and dried fruits as well as the groceries they got in town, he left the cabin door open and dragged Alexander's suitcase behind him further into the cabin. Down the hall, he left the suitcase in the master bedroom, then spent the next little while opening windows and letting the daylight in. The place looked just like he remembered it, its walls loaded with pictures of his family—Mammie, Dad, Donny, his grandmother and grandfather. The furniture was beautiful and old. Most of it they'd had shipped from Puerto Rico and the rest was bought in New York.

In the living room, Augusto descended a couple of steps to the sunroom. He hit the button on the remote and all the blinds slid upward, revealing the lake beyond. The next job was to lift all the white sheets off the furniture and put them away. His mother insisted on covering everything when they would leave to protect it all from dust. Surprisingly, it worked. Not a single stitch of fabric had one fleck of dust on it. He then headed back out to the porch where the second bag was and peered out the door. The front yard had their car, off to the left and straight ahead was nothing but trees.

"Alex?" he called. "Alex, where'd you go?"

"Sorry," Alex called from around the corner of the cabin. When he emerged, he was jogging in a slow sprint. "I had to check it out. Couldn't help myself. This place is gorgeous. So much better than summer in the Hamptons."

Augusto stopped reaching for the suitcase and walked over to sit on one of the porch steps. "Yeah. My grandmother loved it here. It's the only thing we have in our lives that's left of her.

You hungry?"

"Nah." Alex rubbed his stomach. "I think I ate a bag and a half of trail mix." He took a step closer, closing the space between himself and Augusto. "Thank you for sharing this place with me."

"You're welcome." Augusto kissed Alexander's cheek, then his nose, then his lips before wrapping both arms around his hips. "Come inside and see the rest of the place. Are we sharing a room? You know I can easily take the guest room," Augusto teased.

"You're kidding, right?" Alex nipped at his bottom lip, setting free a playful smile. "No way are we sleeping in separate rooms."

"Damn, baby, I was only joking but when you plead your case so vehemently, I have to give in to your…" He trailed off to suck Alex's bottom lip into his mouth. "Every whim."

"Damn, why do you torment me so?" Alex lowered his head. His lips reached Augusto's throat. "Not complaining though. But if you keep on, I swear to God we'll never leave the bed. I don't know about you"—he raised his head to meet Augusto's stare—"but I really want this trip to be more than just lots of sex. It's… important to me."

Augusto kept his gaze for a while, silently reading him. It was a learning experience for Augusto—hearing Alex being sincere still sometimes took him aback. He nodded and tapped Alexander's butt gently. "All right then. Come inside. Let's turn on the AC, grab some juice and you can get the tour. Tomorrow we can go swimming in the lake—it's not a swimming pool so I don't know if you want to be in there—I forgot. What did the doctor say about your foot?"

"The break healed fine. He said I shouldn't have any problems dancing, but suggested I not overdo it for a while." Alex wrapped his hand around Augusto's. They walked back into the house together. "I really want to dance. You have a stereo around here?"

"Yeah." Augusto grinned. "I installed one for my grandmother. She never used it but…" He led Alex through the house to the living room. He hunched down before the elaborate system and pressed the power button. "You can go through the music here and pick something you want."

Alex knelt down beside him and thumbed through a rack of CDs. "I don't recognize any of this stuff. I grew up on classical music and show tunes. I only got to listen to the other stuff when I snuck out of the house. Find something slow...and sexy."

"Slow and sexy he says," Augusto muttered, trailing his index finger over the CDs. Most of the stuff wasn't even in English. Los Exclusivos was a group from Cuba, then there was Shakira, Carlos Santana, Thalia and the list went on and on. Tilting his head, he pushed closer to the floor to inspect the lower shelf and pulled out a CD case that had no writing on it. "What's this?" The question was more for his own thoughts than anything else. Pulling the CD from the case, he plopped it into the player and waited for something to happen. The slow beats of R. Kelling's *Whine for Me* seeped from the speakers and he laughed.

"I know this CD," Augusto said, looking over at Alexander. "You said slow and sexy—you got it."

Alex stood from the floor, holding a hand out for Augusto to take. "I don't even know how to move to this. It's perfect but... except for the show I put on for you at Santo's, I've only ever danced ballet."

"It's not hard." Augusto stood and slowly moved his hips from side to side to the low, reggae-esque beat. "Just let your body feel it."

"My body feels you," Alex whispered, running his hands around Augusto's hips down to lightly grip Augusto's ass. Augusto watched his lover close his eyes, and Alex immediately fell in sync with him, a slow sway of hips that matched the lazy rhythm of the music.

He didn't speak, merely allowed Alex to move with him until he changed the style, almost like changing sexual positions, by adding a slight dip in the movement, causing each shake, each gyration to press their cocks together and rub ever so slightly.

"Roll your hips," Augusto commanded with a gentle voice.

"Mmm...that I can do." Alex grinned wickedly, following through with a dip of hips that made them grind together even harder. Augusto could feel him getting turned on even through both their jeans.

The sexiest thing two lovers could do with each other was dance. That was one of the first lessons on love Augusto had learned from his mother. Though he felt Alexander getting harder and making him aroused as well, he cradled Alexander's face and pressed a kiss to his lover's forehead, remembering Alex's plea about cutting back on the sex. He traced his lips against Alex's forehead, down between his eyes to his nose then brushed them over his lover's lips. The music, the infectious beat made him want to feel Alex in ways he couldn't understand. With his heart beating so fast it drowned the music out from time to time, Augusto pressed closer to his darling, swaying, dipping and rolling their hips together. Electricity surged through him almost bringing a tear to his eye. Instead of giving in to the sensation, he pressed his forehead to Alexander's shoulder.

"Augusto," Alex whispered. "I can't imagine a more perfect time to tell you, I...I love you."

Those three words—those three magical words that ended wars and brought light to darkness. Augusto lifted his head slowly and raked his fingers through his hair. "What did you say?"

"I said I love you." Alex pulled their joined hands up to his lips. "Augusto Catalan, I love you."

"Love me? How do you know?"

"Because there isn't a waking moment I don't think about you. I want to sleep beside you and have you in my arms. I want to see you when you wake up and spend every second of the day with you. I don't want anyone else. I've never thought about anyone else the way I think about you. I...I want you and need you, I don't know how else to explain it. I love you."

"Oh, Alexander..." His voice cracked as he released Alex's hand and caressed the sides of Alex's face. Slowly, he covered

Alex's lips with his. No other man had ever loved him except Kemar. But this time it felt as if he'd conquered the world. Unable to breathe, he lifted his head and met Alex's eyes. "I love you, too…"

Chapter Thirty-four

There wasn't a time Alex could remember hanging on for words like he did with Augusto. He waited, holding his breath for his boyfriend to say those three little magical words back to him, and when Augusto finally did, Alex felt like he was floating.

He curled his fingers around Augusto's and pulled their joined hands between their bodies, holding them close to his heart. Their movement slowed, becoming more of an absent sway than a dance of any sort. Alex caught himself staring, but he couldn't help it. Everything about Augusto was beautiful, and that beauty didn't stop at his looks. It transcended the flesh. Augusto embodied everything Alex considered perfect.

"Should I tell you how relieved I am you said you love me too?"

"But you do know we still have a long ways to go?" Augusto countered.

"Yeah, I know," Alex said, feeling like a lot of the zeal had been sucked out of him. No, he didn't expect them to dive right into being…more, but damn if hearing Augusto say the fact out loud didn't break his spirit a little. "I'll do whatever I need to prove to you I'm sincere, that you're the only person I want. I've never met anyone like you."

"Well, I should hope not. Not everyone can be cursed with this wonderful awesomeness."

Laughing, Alex spun them both around and dipped down to kiss Augusto's jaw. He pushed one hand down his lover's back and pressed Augusto tighter to him. No amount of closeness was enough it seemed.

"I don't think it's a curse at all. I think it's sexy," Alex growled playfully.

"You keep talking like that and I'll never let you leave." Augusto wiggled his brows. The song drew to an end and

Augusto tilted his head. He pressed his lips to the side of Alex's face. "I'm starving."

"You're not talking about starving for me, are you?" Alex responded airily. As Augusto kissed along his neck and jaw, his eyes closed. There was nothing more euphoric than that feeling. "Is it sad that I would rather lie in bed and feed you exotic fruits right now than eat a real meal at a sterile kitchen table?"

"I thought you said this relationship isn't about the sex?" Augusto reminded him.

"Not *just* the sex, but, baby, you can't blame me for getting turned on when you kiss and touch me like that. It's a natural reaction. I'm attracted to you…and so is my body."

Augusto eyed him then laughed softly. "If my body didn't turn you on, there would be something wrong. But why don't we play a game?"

"A game?" Alex quirked a brow. "Should I be worried?"

"I don't know," Augusto replied, taking his hand and pulling the suitcase down the hall. Once there, he sat Alex on the bed and searched his bag, revealing a tie. "I'm going to blindfold you."

"Blindfold?" Alex shook his head. "I don't know, baby…"

Augusto stepped in closer. "Trust me?" he whispered.

"I do."

With those words, he was blindfolded. The next thing he felt was being pulled to his feet. Augusto busied himself with taking all Alex's clothes off until there was nothing but air caressing his body and for a moment after that, Alex neither felt nor heard a thing.

He stood in the middle of the room, totally deprived of his senses. For a moment, Alex had the kind of excitement that made his curiosity fun. But the longer he stood there waiting, the more the excitement turned into worry.

"Augusto?" he called out, just about to reach up and remove the blindfold when a set of warm hands stopped him.

"So, here is the game," Augusto said, softly, trailing a finger down Alex's back. "It's called *where will Augusto put his mouth next?* The only rule—the blindfold must remain on."

"Mmm…" Alex purred. "I think I like the sound of this game."

The first place to get Augusto's lush lips was the small of his back. Hot breath and soft lips flowed over the skin as his Latino lover brushed kisses there. Next, they travelled up his spine, across one shoulder then his neck before Augusto's tongue flicked against the now heated flesh. In a breath, Augusto's mouth was gone only to return, cold with something hard in between, sliding over Alex's back sending a stream of cold water down to the crack of his ass.

Alex hissed, shivering as the coolness rolled over his hot skin. "Jesus, is that ice?" Laughter made his voice quiver.

Augusto didn't reply. The cold merely continued up until it was gone as though it'd melted. The air in the room shifted before the ice came back—this time it was against Alex's abs, down the front of his abdomen, then between his thighs.

Moaning, Alex's head rolled back as his senses burst to life. The cold wasn't distracting anymore. It became a turn on, intoxicating in the way it contrasted the heat of his skin. He spread his legs a little wider and whispered a wavering, "Don't stop."

The cube made its way beneath him, against his balls then to the crack of his ass. Augusto's long fingers pushed the cold between his cheeks before closing the hot flesh over it. His mouth moved on Alex's damp skin, licking and nipping before kissing one of Alex's cheeks.

"I need something to hold on to," Alex said, voice quivering nearly as much as his body. "I swear if I don't, I'll collapse."

"Then hold onto me," Augusto told him, dragging a hand down Alex's side to his thigh. Augusto slipped his arms around him, patting Alex's butt cheeks in tune to an imaginary song.

Holding onto the arm around his waist, Alex stood as best as he could and waited for the next surprise Augusto planned to pull on him. The world was dark from the blindfold and all he had to go by was the sounds in the room and the feel of Augusto moving behind him. He felt his lover slip down his body, trailing kisses over the back of Alex's thighs and each cheek. He felt Augusto's arm dip between his legs and a hand cradling his sac, talented fingers fondling his jewels. Then he felt a tongue slip down the valley of his ass.

CHAPTER THIRTY-FIVE

Augusto smiled, thankful Alexander was taking a chance and doing something a little sexually outrageous. From the other times they'd made love, he knew Alex wasn't really the submissive kind. The moment he saw Alex, he knew the man had a power complex—something that could be a huge turn on in bed and a pain in the ass out of it. Still, he shook his head to clear his mind and continued down his lover's body, stroking the flesh with his tongue and ice cubes. He loved the way the ice melted on Alex, sending trails of water dripping down his back to the wood floor below. Resting a hand on the small of Alex's back, Augusto pushed gently. He felt it the moment Alex hesitated.

"The bed is before you, Alex," Augusto assured his boyfriend. "Just lean forward."

"I trust you," Alex said, leaning forward slowly, hands splayed.

When Augusto was sure Alex was steady on the bed, he pushed his legs open gently and reached for another ice cube. He stuffed it into his mouth while his fingers trailed Alex's crack, stroking the puckered hole that trembled wonderfully. Using the tip of his tongue to lick his own arm, Augusto tested the coldness of his mouth. He was finally satisfied with the ice's effect. His next move was to grip Alex's cheeks in either hand, pulling apart slightly before shoving his tongue into his lover. Alex's hole tensed on his cold tongue then trembled. It was the reaction Augusto was looking forward to and then some. He groaned, lashing his tongue back and forth then used it as he would his cock. Slipping the tip into Alex, he gripped his lover's hips and pulled his ass back to stick his tongue deeper.

"Holy shit," Alex breathed, pressing his ass out even farther. "I've…I've…Never…Oh, God."

But Augusto didn't let up. He clung to Alex's writhing body, tasted from him, pushed his pleasure and drank his fill. Grabbing another cube, he slid it over Alex for a moment then used his now warm mouth to suck the cold away. Alex trembled against him and for a moment he thought for sure something was wrong. That was until Alex reached back and grabbed his hair. Augusto braced his arm across Alex's back, unhooked his lover's fingers from his curls and pulled back.

"Tell me where else you want my mouth," he demanded from Alex. When all Alex did was moan, Augusto spanked him. "Come on, Alex. Be a good boy and tell me where you want my mouth."

"On my…On my…" Alex panted. It took a second for him to catch his breath. "On my cock."

A smirk passed Augusto's lips but he turned Alex around and laid him on the bed. He pressed Alex's hands down. "Keep your hands here. No matter what, you can't touch me."

Augusto kissed his way down Alex's body until he was face-to-face with Alex's cock. He moved closer to it, allowing his breath to trace the hard shaft but didn't put his mouth on it. For the time being he licked at Alex's balls, sucking them into his mouth and playing them over his tongue. The sound of Alex breathing hard turned him on even more, made his body pulse sweetly. Augusto welcomed that feeling of life within him, driving him. Sliding upward, he dragged his tongue along Alex's shaft, feeling it throb against his lips. He gave Alex what he wanted, pushing the dick down his throat while tickling the base with the very tip of his tongue.

The sound of Alex's moans warmed Augusto's being. He raised his stare to find Alex gripping the bed linens so hard his knuckles had turned white. "You have the most talented tongue."

Sucking a finger wet, Augusto inserted it inside Alexander, slowly at first as he worked to open Alex up. Then, he moved it in rhythm to his suction. Pre-cum dripped into his mouth causing Augusto to moan, feeling his cock pushing against the material of his clothes. It wanted to be released but this wasn't about him. He wanted to get Alex off, to watch the way his eyes widened and his beautiful pink lips spread in nothing but pleasure as he exploded. Augusto wanted to feel Alex's cum burn into his mouth, pushing him toward the edge. Groaning, he sucked harder, driving his finger deeply into his boyfriend's body.

Alex bucked, moaned and shouted his name. But the most beautiful sound to leave his lips was his confession of love repeatedly. It was as though once he said it he just couldn't stop himself. Augusto felt an overwhelming fire surge through him. It only magnified when Alex finally gripped his hair, against Augusto's rules. Still, he would punish him later. He busied himself trying to make Alex come for him.

"That's it. Keep going," Alex begged, rolling his hips and making love to Augusto's mouth. Purrs, moans, and sounds that had no words rumbled up through Alex's excited body. Sweat blossomed on his skin. "I'm about…I'm about…Oh, God. Holy…" His voice trailed off into one of the wildest moans Augusto had ever heard from a lover.

Lifting his mouth, he was rewarded with a large burst of hot liquid against his neck, against the tip of his nose. He laughed softly, stroking Alex's cock to get every last bit out against his skin. Alex writhed against the bed, sexily in a way, sending Augusto's lust into overdrive. Snaking up Alex's body, he pulled the blindfold from his lover's eyes and looked down into his face. "Hi…"

"I've made a mess of you," Alex said, voice hoarse and raspy. He reached up and brushed his thumb over Augusto's nose, then licked the spill from his fingertip.

"My mother always told me to clean up after myself." Augusto kissed him deeply. "What do you think?"

"I think that was the most incredible thing I've ever experienced." Alex leaned up and licked the pearly spend from Augusto's neck, kissing along the way.

Breathing became an issue for Augusto but he bowed to kiss the top of Alex's head. "*Te mereces buen amor*," Augusto whispered.

"I don't know what that means, but it sounds beautiful the way you say it."

"*Te mereces buen amor*," Augusto repeated, pressing a hand to Alex's chest and pushing him gently back to the bed. "It means…

you deserve good love…"

"I have good love. You." Alex touched Augusto's face. "You're the best love I could've asked for."

Augusto smiled at Alex. "I'm glad to hear that. Let's see how you feel after a few days cooped up in this cabin with me."

"I couldn't imagine a better way to spend a weekend, Augusto. I mean that." Alex reached around to grip the back of Augusto's neck, then he pulled gently. "Now, make love to me."

CHAPTER THIRTY-SIX

With a groan, Alex flopped over in the bed. After the marathon sex they'd had last night, he found himself drained of energy, and muscles he didn't know existed ached. They'd done soft and sweet, rough and quick. He'd even let Augusto bind his hands—something Alex never thought he would *ever* enjoy. He found out he did, a hell of a lot more than he'd imagined.

He rolled over in the bed and found it empty; the sheets cool as if Augusto had been gone for a while. It was a jarring way to wake up, to know the person he'd fallen asleep beside was no longer there. The discovery of the empty bed stopped his heart for a split second.

Alex dragged in a deep breath as he brushed his hair back from his face. It was then he smelled hickory-smoked bacon and the scent of something freshly baked, like bread or biscuits. A smile curled his lips. He knew Augusto liked to cook, but never expected him to get up and make breakfast alone.

Climbing out of the bed, he was excited to share their first breakfast together. It was the way Alex dreamed of waking up every day for the rest of his life. Well, in Augusto's arms first, then breakfast and showers and rushing off to school or work together. With the smile still on his lips, he made his way into the living room and toward the kitchen, but didn't find his lover or the first trace of food. His smile quickly turned to a frown. He called out Augusto's name, but his boyfriend didn't answer. He called again. Still nothing.

When Alex crossed into the kitchen, he caught sight of a shadow moving around on the porch at the back of the house. The French door was propped open, leaving nothing but a screen between him and the great outdoors. He called Augusto's name again, and this time his lover acknowledged him.

Alex stepped out onto the porch and found a spread fit for a king laid out on the picnic table. There were scrambled eggs and piles of bacon, biscuits and freshly squeezed orange juice, but the best sight of all was Augusto smiling proudly, with his hands on both hips. Alex approached him and stole a chaste kiss.

"Have you been up since the break of dawn?" he asked.

"You would think so, wouldn't you?" Augusto replied. "Here, sit down."

Alex sat down exactly where Augusto told him to. Augusto sat down beside him and started passing around plates. It was a far cry from the power bars and coffee Alex had become accustomed to in his years of bachelorhood. Save for the fat and carbs, he could get used to this real fast.

"You really didn't have to go through all this trouble, baby. I'm thankful, but I could've helped or…something."

"Would you relax?" Augusto handed Alex a cold glass of orange juice. "I was trying to do something nice for you. Enjoy it."

"It's perfect." Alex leaned over and kissed Augusto's cheek before popping a piece of bacon in his mouth.

"After a few hours, we'll go for a swim to work off all this food we're eating right now." Augusto grinned, reaching for a sausage. "I don't think Luther would be happy if I showed up at Santo's looking like I gained a house."

"Sweetie, Santo's would be the least of your worries. You haven't seen the teachers at Julliard with the kids they consider 'fat'." Alex air-quoted the word. "You should've seen Margot when Carolynne broke up with her boyfriend and gained like six pounds. It was *ug-ly*."

"I'll bet. But this weekend is not about sadness. We can deal with all that at some point when we go back to the madness. Jason seems to be taking it well but Julliard is tough." Augusto took a breath and bit off a piece of the sausage and chewed. He glanced out over the water. "Before my father died, he would bring us here every weekend no matter what. I think we only missed one weekend and that was because my mother had to go down to the Children's Aid to sign some papers for my brother."

Alex frowned. He scooped a bit of eggs into his mouth as he thought about what Augusto said. "Children's Aid? What...does that mean?" He held up a hand. "If I'm prying, tell me it's none of my business."

Augusto shook his head. "My brother Donny...I don't know if you've seen the picture of the very large black man in the living room? That's my brother. He was adopted because my mother was told by the doctors she couldn't have any more children—she wasn't even supposed to have me."

"I saw the picture, but I didn't know...are you guys close?"

"Donny and I?" Augusto questioned then nodded. "Yeah. He's always had my back. He went away to fight the war on terror and I just about died."

"But he came home, right?"

"Thankfully. He came back just as I started Julliard. Two of my three miracles this year." Augusto chuckled. "I said miracles—my father would have been so proud."

"Miracles? What's your third miracle?"

"You." Augusto said the word as though it was a prayer. He turned to meet Alex's eyes. "You are my third miracle this year."

Admittedly, Alex wasn't expecting that, but when Augusto said it, Alex felt the fluttering of true happiness ripple through him. The feeling elicited a genuine smile. No one had ever called Alex a miracle—not his parents, not the man he'd once thought he loved. No one. It was at that moment Alex realized just how deeply he loved Augusto.

"You're a very lucky man. No one has ever cared enough to call me a miracle," Alex said softly, turning his face back to his plate. "You've been loved all your life, by your mom and dad, and siblings and friends. You were probably even loved unconditionally by a significant other, weren't you?"

Augusto went silent. Alex heard the moment Augusto inhaled and pushed the air out of his mouth. "Yes. His name was Kemar—Luther's son. Luther owns Santo's."

It didn't take a mind reader to see Kemar had had a significant impact on Augusto's life. Alex could tell by the change in Augusto's expression and the darkening of his eyes that Kemar was still very important to Augusto. Alex scooted across the bench, closing the slight space between the two of them. He wrapped his hand over Augusto's.

"What happened? Why aren't you still with him?"

"Ah…" Augusto's voice cracked. He cleared his throat, pushed his food away from him and ran a hand over the back of his neck. "We were together for a couple of years. He was the head dancer at Santo's. You know how they say there's no such thing as perfection? They never met Kemar—he and his love for me were perfect. He was fine, healthy—then he started getting tired all the time. There was no one in that whole business who would beat him to Santo's. Every day he'd be there so for a while I thought, he was just burned out. But it got worse. When I finally talked him into going to the doctor they told him he had prostate cancer."

"Oh, God, Augusto…" Alex paused, squeezing his lover's hand tighter. "Did he die?"

"Alex…" Augusto pushed up from where he was sitting. He faced the water, back hunched slightly. He raked his fingers through his hair. "He died a few months later. They didn't catch it in time. There's nothing they could have done. He was so young! At first I thought, *'This is a mistake! It has to be a mistake!'* Then his health just deteriorated and I was so angry and all I could think was—*this isn't fair.*"

The need to run to Augusto and pull him into his arms took Alex over, but as badly as he wanted to do that, it seemed like Augusto just needed space. It was one of those awkward moments when a person became torn between their needs and the needs of the one they loved to the very depths of their being. The only thing Alex could manage was a quiet, "I'm so sorry."

And Alex suddenly understood why being the only one had been so important to Augusto. The other man had been surrounded by love, by deep relationships all his life. It's all he knew and all he wanted. Alex had been raised very differently, by people who were paid to care, entertained by teachers and nannies and toys and…things. But now that Augusto had come into his life and showed him what love, true love, felt like, Alex couldn't imagine anything different.

He pushed up to his feet and crossed the porch, standing close behind his lover but not crowding him. He said, "Thank you for giving me a chance with your heart. I'll do my best to treat it with care."

"He loved me, Alex," Augusto spoke. His voice was gravelly and low. "He didn't have to say it. I could feel it whenever he touched me. I felt it whenever he stared at me when he thought I wasn't looking. At nights when he thought I was asleep, he would play the piano in the living room and I'd just lay there smiling. He had this voice that just made everything wonderful again. I'm not saying all this to make you feel cheap or unloved. I'm telling you this so you know, I've been loved deeply before and I know what it's supposed to feel like."

"You don't feel that with me, do you?" Alex asked, and soon as he said the words, his heart sunk.

Augusto turned then and cradled Alex's face. "What I feel for you is different than what I felt for Kemar. It was a different time and a different love. I feel something strong and desperate for you, Alex—please understand even though it's not the same, it's just as intense."

"I don't expect you to love me the same way, just…love me, okay? I don't think I could handle it if you didn't."

"Oh, darling," Augusto said, pulling Alex into his arms. "I love you like you wouldn't believe."

Alex buried his head against Augusto's shoulder and took a deep breath. He held his boyfriend as tight as he could, knowing there was no way in hell he could ever let Augusto go, not without a fight.

"I love you like you wouldn't believe, too."

CHAPTER THIRTY-SEVEN

Augusto was enjoying the day with Alexander more than he thought he could. Most times he merely sat back, arm behind his head, either on the hammock in the sunroom or on the porch and watched Alex. Sometimes he went quiet, thinking of what he was possibly getting himself into. Still, he silenced those thoughts and breathed. From time to time Alex caught him staring and his cheeks would heat up—something Augusto found so damn cute his heart would race uncontrollably. Other times he merely walked over and covered Alex's lips with his. For some reason he was starving for this man and he just didn't want to be careful anymore.

Sunday morning was rolling in with slight rain when Augusto opened his eyes. He could hear the softness of water flowing down the window. This time he didn't climb out of bed like he would have but stayed with Alex who was cuddled into his chest and sleeping. He dropped a kiss to his lover's head, not because he wanted to, but because he just didn't have a choice. The reality of them having to go back to the city was sinking in and left Augusto with a strange, wilting feeling inside.

He held Alex tighter. "Baby?" he called softly, moving his mouth along Alex's hairline.

"Mhm…?" Alex half-groaned, slowly peeling his eyes open. A smile curled his lips when Augusto kissed his forehead again.

"I thought you were going to sleep the day away," Augusto teased. "It's our last day here. We should do something."

Alex barely lifted his head, turning toward the bedroom window. "Sounds like rain. What can we do that doesn't involve going outside?"

"I'm glad you asked," Augusto replied, kissing him quickly and pushing himself up from the bed. He walked over to the dresser and pulled out the lowest drawer. From that, he grabbed an old decorative box and carried it back to the bed. "We can do this."

Alex arched a brow, caution written all over his face. "And what exactly is *this*?"

"Whenever anyone visits the cabin—they have to write something they find special about the place and put it into this box." Augusto opened it, dug through the folded pieces of papers inside and pulled out a small notepad and a pencil. "Once it's full, we'll carry it out to Nana's favorite spot on the land and bury the papers."

"What if I found the most special thing about this place before we ever arrived?" Alex said as he sat up on the bed. He fingered a piece of paper for a moment, as if he was deep in thought. Then his eyes widened and he said, "Actually, I know what to write."

"I don't get to see what you write," Augusto assured him. "This is between you and Nana."

"You're not curious?"

"Yes. But it's against the rules to share." Augusto eyed him for a moment. Of course he wanted to see what one of the only two men he'd ever taken to Nana's cabin had to say. But his mother had created the rule so the note would make Nana smile—as strange as it sounded.

"If those are the rules," Alex said, and he reached for a pen and a piece of paper. He started scribbling on the page occasionally looking up, catching Augusto watching him write.

Augusto wrote something, stopped, ripped the paper up into tiny pieces then tried again. For a moment he stared at the scrawled words and folded his paper. He tilted his head. "Are we writing an essay?"

"I have a lot to say. This trip was…" Alex's voice trailed off and he went back to writing.

"I see," Augusto replied. He dropped his note into the box and climbed from the bed. "Let me know when you're finished. I need something to eat."

"You mind grabbing me a cup of coffee?" Alex asked without raising his head.

"Sure."

Augusto left him there scribbling away and entered the kitchen. The rain poured down the glass windows as he set up the coffeemaker. While he waited he dropped a few waffles into a pan and grabbed a couple of plates from the cupboard. The thought of what Alex could possibly be writing danced through his head but rules were rules. He would respect them. Inhaling a deep breath, he dug through what was left of their groceries in the fridge and found some blueberries. By the time the coffee was ready, so were the waffles. He dressed them with syrup and blueberries then carried a plate, fork and a cup of coffee into the bedroom.

"All right Stephen King, eat something," he teased.

"All finished." Alex beamed as he stuffed the paper into the box. "I feel like I just had a confessional with a priest." He reached for the plate.

"To be a fly on that wall." Augusto handed over the goods before fetching his and sitting on the edge of the bed. "The weekend isn't long enough."

"No. It really isn't. I don't know how I'm going to sleep without you softly snoring in my ear or absently stroking my chest. It's going to suck."

Augusto laughed. "I don't snore!"

Alex gave him a droll expression. "Yeah, baby, you do."

"Don't look at me like that." Augusto snorted with mirth. "I don't care what you say, I'm not a snoring person."

"Either way." Alex laughed. "Sleeping without you will suck."

Augusto nodded. "It'll be all right. It's only until we figure out what we are doing."

"I know what I'm doing and I know what I want."

"You know what I mean."

"Yeah, I do, but Augusto"—Alex took his hand—"you're it for me. I think, at least to me, what we're doing is clear."

"I know I love you, Alex. There's nothing unsure about that. But my life is a lot less comfortable and I want to be able to provide for you."

"*I* can provide for both of us. You can work and all of that, but…" Alex exhaled. "I want you to live with me."

"Think about that for a second. Do you think it would make me happy having you provide for me?"

"No, but—"

"I need to work, Alex. We can make plans later. We're still in school. Once we're finished then we can figure out the rest of this. In the meantime—we're going to make this work."

"I know you're right, and I want you to be happy, but I want you to be with me too." Alex stood from the bed and collected their soiled dishes. "Just know that's where my heart and head are. I'm serious about us."

Reaching up, Augusto caressed his arm. "I know, sweetie."

CHAPTER THIRTY-EIGHT

The apartment smelled of fresh pine and baked ham—the staples of any wintery holiday feast. Keith—Augusto's longtime friend and one of Alex's new roomies—was in the kitchen cooking a small feast. Augusto worked on the pomp and fanfare for their Christmas celebration. Alex was a nervous wreck and even having Carolynne by his side didn't make things better.

He and Augusto had been dating since late summer, and they had yet to do the whole "meet the parents" thing with either side. Alex's parents were somewhere in Europe for the winter, as per usual, and who knew when they would be back, let alone care enough to meet the man their son loved. Because of Alex's issues with family, love, and being surrounded by people who cared, he'd asked Augusto to hold off with any plans for them all to get together. Carolynne had berated him about how ridiculous he'd been acting, how good men believed in family and if Alex didn't meet Augusto's soon, he might very well lose the love of his life.

Before they knew it, months had passed and winter was upon them. They skirted through Thanksgiving, choosing to go their separate ways for the time being, and that went over just fine. But when Augusto had told Alex, "Mammie and Donny want to have Christmas with us, they want to meet you, and they won't take no for an answer,"—Alex had no choice but to surrender…on the condition they make their relationship as official as it could be without getting married. They moved in together, which of course came with the condition that Keith lived there too.

No problem. For Augusto, anything.

Alex was in the room he and his boyfriend shared, wrapping a few small last minute gifts for Carolynne and Kenny—the only people he really considered his friends. His hands trembled so badly he could barely cut the wrapping paper, and the stupid contraption meant to make perfect edges just wasn't working the way it should have.

He crossed the hall into the one office the three of them shared, went to the desk and started rooting around for a real pair of scissors. In his digging, a letter from the school fell out onto the floor.

Frowning, Alex bent over and picked it up, not remembering anything the school had sent to the apartment since it all went to his father's office in Manhattan. He unfolded the page slowly. In big red letters at the top were the words, "Final notice." He read through it, thinking something had to be horribly wrong, and that's when he found it was addressed to Augusto. Apparently, his lover was on the verge of getting kicked out of school for not paying his tuition.

Alex's heart sank in his chest. If Augusto didn't go to Juilliard, then what would become of his dreams? What would become of them as a couple? Would Augusto leave him?

No. No. No.

He peeked his head into the living room. Carolynne and Augusto were working on something near the tree. They were both in the middle of laughing. Alex said, "Baby, come here for a minute. I need your help," before heading back into their bedroom.

"Gimme a sec," Augusto called. Soon he stuck his head into the room. "Yeah?"

Alex sat down on the edge of the bed and held out the letter. "Found this in the desk," he said in a calm, soft voice despite his wanting to fall apart. "What are you going to do?"

Augusto stepped in and took the paper from his hand to read it. Instantly, Alex saw his eyes change. "Don't worry about it, Alex." Augusto stressed the words by crumpling the letter in his fist.

"Don't worry about it?" Alex tilted his head, frowning up at Augusto. "They're going to kick you out of school. How can you tell me not to worry?"

"Because what good is worrying going to do?" Augusto snapped. "There is nothing you can do about it other than give yourself a hernia."

"That's not true. I could've…I don't know. I could've helped you figure this out."

Augusto touched the side of Alex's face. "Baby, listen to me. I knew you would want to help. That's why I didn't tell you. I didn't mean to snap, I just—it's a lot of weight on my shoulders right now and I know how important this is, but if the money isn't there, it isn't there. I may have to take time off or something but it's just the way it is. Don't worry. It's almost Christmas."

"I am worried about it." Alex's voice turned pleading. "Please, let me help you. Please."

"Unless you plan on winning the lottery." Augusto chuckled. "Please, don't worry. I'll figure this out. I always do."

"Baby, you don't have time to just 'figure this out.' That was the final notice."

"And I know that. Just leave it be. Please. Let me handle this."

"Fine. Whatever. Just…please don't let this come between us. I don't want to lose you."

"Why would this come between us?" Augusto sounded genuinely confused.

"I'm just afraid you not being in school might…I don't know, put distance between us."

"Did I not tell you I'm not going anywhere? I meant that. Now, as sexy as I think you are walking around this room without pants, my mother and brother are due soon—so put some on." Augusto kissed him chastely, then made a sound in his throat before reaching in for a more meaningful kiss.

The kiss broke, but Alex didn't feel any better about the conversation. He knew his lover wouldn't ask anyone for help and that Augusto would drop out before he willingly took a handout. Alex also knew if he handled it without Augusto's permission, there would be hell to pay. It was a lose-lose situation.

The door closed with a startling thud. He heard Carolynne, Keith and Augusto talking in the other room. Then he heard voices he didn't recognize. It was time to put on his happy face, push back his worry, and meet his lover's family.

He pulled his Marc Jacobs dress slacks up to his waist and fastened his belt, then slipped into a soft cashmere sweater in a shade of blue that complemented his eyes well. Looking in the mirror, he was pleased with what he saw. His face was clean-shaven and his hair styled to perfection. Surely they would be impressed. Surely his lover's family would like him as much as Augusto did as long as he didn't get nervous and make a complete fool of himself.

The bedroom door cracked open and Carolynne poked her head in. She seemed hesitant and maybe a little concerned. Alex hated the idea of her worrying about him. "Everyone is here," she said softly. "Are you okay?"

"I'm fine."

"You don't look fine."

Alex squared his shoulders, looked himself over in the mirror again, then he exhaled and his body deflated. "I'll be fine. I just… I'm doing me, you know?"

"Boy, don't I ever?"

"I'm going to run him off. I know I will, Carolynne."

"He loves you, Alex. That's obvious. So if he does run, he won't run far."

"I don't want him to run at all."

Chapter Thirty-nine

"You're losing too much weight," Augusto's mother complained, poking him with her finger as he handed her a glass. "They're working you too hard over at that school."

Augusto laughed. "No, Mammie," he replied, then lifted the front of his shirt to show his mother his abs. "I just lost a few pounds but the rest is muscle. It's a good thing."

"When I was your age, I loved my man with meat on his bones." She shrugged before sipping from her glass.

Keith, Donny and Jason were laughing so hard Augusto thought for sure they would pass out. Augusto kissed the side of her head and she smiled lovingly at him, caressed his cheek then stood. "Okay, let me see the kitchen," she said.

"No." He switched to Spanish. "You're our guest. We made enough food to feed everyone. Stop worrying so much."

Donny, who was fiddling with the sound system looked up, waving a CD at Augusto. "What's this? Porn?"

Augusto's cheeks heated. "No. It's music for my ballet class."

Donny smirked, shook his head and grabbed another CD. Augusto watched as Donny shoved the tray in and soft music began playing. Donny could never do anything without music. Augusto reached out and helped his brother up as Keith began bringing food to the table.

"You want some help?" Augusto asked.

"I'll help him." Jason shoved to his feet while looking toward the bedroom. He was smiling and Augusto really hated when Jason got a certain look in his eyes. That meant he was up to something. His suspicions were confirmed when he followed Jason's eyes to see Alexander standing there. Carolynne slipped out from behind him and went to join the others in the kitchen. Augusto felt so weak in that moment, he knew the only thing to help him was a kiss from the man he'd grown to feel so strongly for.

"Mammie, there's someone I'd like you to meet." He extended a hand to Alex.

Alex gave them a soft, nervous smile. Keith wolf whistled in the background and Alex turned the most adorable shade of red. He reached for Mammie's hand and said, "Welcome to our home, Mrs. Catalan. It's so nice to finally meet you."

"Oh, Augusto, he's darling!" Mammie cheered, shaking Alexander's hand then turning him slightly. "But you should feed him more."

Augusto smirked mischievously at Alex until Donny spoke. "She didn't mean *that* feeding!"

"Why do you always have to be such a pervert?" Augusto asked.

Everyone let out a riotous laugh.

"Now behave." Mammie chuckled. "Do you see what I have to put up with?" She was speaking to Alex now. "It's nice to meet you. You've made my son very happy."

"Mammie…"

"Don't shush me child." She batted a wrist at him. "I only speak the truth."

"Your son has made *me* very happy." Alex shot a faint smile over his shoulder to Augusto. "He's rather wonderful," he said without looking away.

Augusto noticed the proud way his mother beamed but shook his head and walked off into the kitchen to help Keith and Carolynne. He only succeeded with being handed a large pitcher of juice.

"Don't drop it," Keith told him. "Now shoo."

Muttering a profanity under his breath he carried it out and placed it on the center of the table and took one of the chairs. Alex and his mother were already in a deep conversation and, from experience, he knew that was never any good. It wasn't that his mother hated Kemar or Alex—from what he could see—it was that when she liked one of his boyfriends, she would regale them with childhood stories. They were all tales that made Augusto want to bury his head in the dirt—stories like when he rode the dog around the yard at four in the nude.

"He was actually naked," he heard his mother saying.

Augusto banged his forehead slowly into the table.

Alex chuckled. When the laughter died down, something solemn came over him. He said, "I don't think my parents could tell any stories like this. It's not that I didn't pull my pranks, it's just…"

"Well, don't worry. Stick with this family long enough and we'll have stories to tell about you." Mammie grinned.

By then the table was set and everyone was sitting. Augusto knew Keith was a genius when it came to the kitchen so he wasn't surprised that everything looked good, and smelled even better. He often asked why Keith had chosen to be a cop and not a chef. Each time Keith would simply shrug and say he could do both. That was the truth.

"All right people, let's hold hands and grace the table," Donny called, reaching for their mother's hand.

Augusto sat between Carolynne and Alex, gripping their hands. Just before closing his eyes, he kissed Alex's fingers.

Donny said grace and when he was finished, Augusto watched silently as his new family helped themselves to dinner. He didn't feel quite hungry but the energy around him made it impossible to want to leave this peaceful place. With so many things weighing on his mind from his exhaustion with a relationship, work, school, family—everything was too much. But if he wanted things to work, if he wanted his dreams he had to fight for them. Augusto glanced at Carolynne and wondered what she thought of him and her best friend being together. She caught him staring so he smiled and turned to what was happening around the table. The conversations around him swirled about his head like images on a screen. From time to time he smiled at something as the others erupted in laughter but didn't contribute to the conversation.

He managed to dish some food out for himself and ate slowly, wondering how he'd gotten so lucky. Even with all the worries, he had a man who loved him, a mother who adored him, a brother and friends who supported him. It felt good to have. With a quick glance over at Jason, Augusto took a breath, knowing his friend's situation. Jason had no family in the United States. After he explained that, Augusto invited him to stay for Christmas and was very glad when Jason accepted.

"I got a little gift for everyone," Alex said. Augusto raised his head, shock filling his face. "It's nothing huge or expensive, just…sentimental, since this is my first of hopefully many, many Christmases with you all."

Alex stood from his chair and headed straight over to the tree. He grabbed gift bags—one for each person at the table, even Jason, whom he didn't know so well. He handed Mammie a bag first. She opened it slowly and said, "You shouldn't have gone to the trouble."

"Oh, it was no trouble at all. I love shopping and I've never had a real holiday with family, so…"

"Well, that's a shame," she said. She lifted a small black box from the bag and opened it. Inside was a white gold necklace with an open heart pendant. "This is beautiful, Alexander."

"It's from me *and* Augusto."

The feeling of being punched in the chest left Augusto gasping silently for air. He pushed from the table and headed for the door.

"Gus!" Keith called.

"What's wrong?" Jason was next.

"I'm fine. I can't breathe!" Augusto called.

Donny was by his side, clutching his shoulders. "Gus, look at me."

He fought to obey. He locked eyes with his brother, who now cradled his face. "He's fine," Donny explained. "Just in shock.

Alex, you wanna take him into the bedroom for a second?"

Augusto locked eyes with Alex and Alex immediately paled. "Sure," Alex said, caution and wariness spilling into his voice. He waited as Augusto stalked past him, then followed him into the bedroom. "I screwed up, didn't I?" Alex asked.

Augusto said nothing. He merely stared out the window with his arms folded over his chest. His lungs still burned slightly and it felt as though the meal was sitting on his chest, weighing him down. "No…" his voice was so soft he wasn't sure if he'd spoken.

"You're lying to me."

"Why would you think I'm lying to you?"

"Because, I know that look. You're upset. I just gave your mother a beautiful necklace and you're upset. Naturally, with me." Augusto heard him exhale sharply. "Maybe I should just go for a bit. The cool air might do some good. You can have the apartment to yourself, with your family."

Augusto walked over to their dresser and pulled out a small box with a tiny lock on it. "Have you ever wondered what's in this?"

"Sometimes." Alex shrugged. "I assumed if you wanted me to know you would tell me."

"I know I should get rid of it. I know it could hurt you but I feel like I'm letting him down if I do…" Trailing off, Augusto gripped the small lock and yanked hard. There was a sharp wrenching sound before the lock snapped and he let it fall to the ground. He opened the small box and pulled out a silver necklace with an open heart pendant. "The day Kemar died—he gave me this. Aside from Santo's and Luther this is all I have left of years of my life."

All the color in Alex's skin faded away. He sank down on the edge of the bed—mouth agape, eyes wide. "I…Jesus, Augusto, I didn't know. I couldn't have known. I—"

"It's all right." Augusto hugged Alex tightly. "It's fine, I swear. I was just taken by surprise. I don't mean to hide things from you and this is the last one, I swear. But I didn't know how to tell you. I never want to lose you, do you understand?"

Alex nodded slowly, mouth still hanging wide open. "I really am sorry. I—" Augusto pressed his finger to Alex's lips.

"I just need you to hold me right now. Please…"

Without having to be told twice, Alex wrapped his arms around Augusto's waist and buried his face in the curve of Augusto's stomach. He held on tight, tighter than Augusto had ever felt him embrace him before. Then he heard a muffled, "I love you so much."

A relieved breath passed his lips and all the troubles in the world seemed to melt with those words. He smiled, caressing the back of Alex's head. "I have a gift for you too. It's still under the tree."

"You ready to go back out there?"

"Wait a second," Augusto replied, sinking down to kiss Alex. "Now I'm ready."

Alex gave him a thoroughly genuine smile, then rose from the bed. As they walked out of the room to join the rest of the family, Alex kept one arm around Augusto, even when the whistles and catcalls started up again. It was Mammie who put an end to the other guys' teasing. "You all stop that, now," she said.

"You fools. I can't take them anywhere," Augusto said but he was grinning. He stopped by the tree and picked up a small wrapped gift and handed it to Alex. "Open this one first."

Augusto watched as Alex carefully unwrapped the small box. He was the kind of guy who took time to slip his fingers under the edges so he wouldn't make a mess of the paper. The suspense—even though Augusto already knew what was hiding behind the silvery paper—was enough to make him want to run across the space and rip open the gift himself.

Next was a smaller box. Augusto watched his boyfriend's hands shake as he pulled the top off the small box to reveal a ring—a simple gold band, shined to glisten in the light of the room. For that instant, it felt as if he couldn't breathe but he didn't care. His eyes, mind and everything in him focused on what was happening, on the tremble of Alexander's hand and the way his lips spread slightly. The room became silent, like no one else existed but the two of them and his heart hammered almost painfully inside his chest.

"Marry me?" Augusto questioned.

The gasp that spilled from Alex's lips was in complete harmony with the gasps filling the air behind them. He had the same wide-eyed, surprised face he'd had in the bedroom, but this time there was a light to it.

"Are you…? You really…?" Alex frowned as he looked up at Augusto. "You're serious?"

"Say yes!" Carolynne blurted.

"Say yes!" Donny, Keith and Jason agreed.

"Would you hobos cut it out!" Augusto called. "Stop pressuring him! And yes, I'm serious."

"Yes, I'll…I'll marry you."

"Yeah?" Augusto asked, stepping in to wrap his arms around Alex. The others cheered but he wasn't really paying them any attention. "You're not just saying yes because these nerds are pressuring you?"

"No." Alex smiled, finally relaxing so much his shoulders rounded. "No, I'm saying yes because I love you and there's no one on this planet I could ever want more than I want you."

Augusto tossed his head back and laughed. There was no happier feeling he could ever remember coming close to this. Cradling Alex's face, he kissed his nose then forehead before his mother walked over to them.

"That's your father's ring," she whispered.

"Yes, Mammie."

"Can I?" She asked, her voice soft.

Augusto nodded and she pulled the ring from the box.

Picking up Alex's hand, Augusto watched his mother slip the ring on Alex's finger. "This ring once belonged to a man who I loved dearly and who Gus thought the sun rose and set with. It's only fitting you now wear it."

"I'm so honored," Alex said. His eyes turned glassy and he started to blink rapidly. Once the ring was settled onto his hand, he curled his fingers and held his fist to his heart. "I'm...I'm... speechless." He laughed.

CHAPTER FORTY

After dinner, Augusto needed some air. He was so full he didn't have the energy the others had to play video games. After they retired to the living room, he spent the next few minutes stocking the dishwasher and starting it. He started the kettle to make himself another cup of tea—this time green tea—and leaned his back into the counter. Kemar floated into his mind then and he wondered if he could really, truly be happy with Alex. But then he felt silly for he was happy with Alex. He felt such overwhelming joy waking up in Alex's arms, he almost felt guilty about being so free.

"Are you coming?" Jason wanted to know.

"Nah," Augusto said, turning to look at his friend. "I'm going to grab some tea and sit on the balcony for a while. I'm too full for anything but that."

Jason laughed. "All right—but your loss."

Augusto grinned and Jason left him alone then just as the kettle started whistling. He poured some water into the teapot, picked up his favorite mug, hooked it over a finger, stuck a spoon between his lips and reached for the teapot. Augusto balanced everything as he made his way out to the balcony and after setting his treasures down, he settled in one of the comfortable padded chairs. Closing his eyes, he inhaled. There was something marvelous on the air. Perhaps it was because he had all the people he cared for in one space and they sounded like they were enjoying themselves immensely together. But no matter the reason, he was thankful—blissful. While he set up his tea, another burst of excitement filled the air from inside.

"Hey! Cheater!" Keith accused.

"It's not my fault you suck at this!" Jason replied.

Augusto chuckled, curling his legs beneath him and lifting his tea to his lips. Keith sucked at video games. To him the winners always cheated.

"Boys. So noisy," Carolynne grumbled. She stepped out onto the balcony, sliding the glass door closed behind her.

Augusto turned. "I know. Boys can be such pains."

She sat down on the chair beside him and pulled her legs up to her chest. Augusto caught her glancing over like she wanted to express something monumental to him, but didn't quite know how to say it.

"Okay," Augusto said, taking a sip from his cup and placing it on the glass table. "I'll bite. What is it?"

He heard her inhale sharply, then she turned almost her entire body in the chair. "You're going to take care of him, right? I mean, like…I don't have to worry about you hurting him, do I?"

For a moment, Augusto simply stared at her as if she wasn't speaking English. He then looked out at the view before them and took a breath. "If I didn't love him, we wouldn't be here right now," he replied simply. "I have no intentions of hurting him."

"Okay." She nodded. "I have to be honest, Gus. I wanted him to end up with my brother, but they're…too different. They didn't do it for each other, not like you do it for him. I'm not sure how to explain it, but something changed in him when he got with you. He softened…in a good way. I like it."

"Well, that's precisely what a guy wants to hear the best friend say about the fiancé." He reached for his tea.

Carolynne blinked. "Do you mean that, or was it sarcasm?"

"I was being sarcastic." Augusto rolled his shoulders. "I know I don't have the money Alex has or the family influence. I don't have any of that. But all I want from Alex is his love and his heart. I spent my whole life without being wealthy and I managed perfectly fine. You didn't say it but I know what you were thinking."

"I honestly wasn't, Augusto. I love him to death, but he was an ass sometimes. He's changed for the better. And my brother is happier too, so it worked out. Don't you think it worked out?"

"Ass?" Augusto chuckled. "That wasn't the word I'd have used to describe him. I must admit when I found out about your brother I hit the roof. The last thing I wanted to be was *the other man*. I'm still not quite sure what kind of relationship they had but if he's okay then yes, it worked out."

"Kenny and Alex were never serious. It started because we'd all been sitting around drinking one night, and we were talking about not having boyfriends. One thing led to another and I was on the couch alone while Alex and Kenny were in his bedroom. They were safe for each other." Carolynne shrugged. "They weren't attached and didn't have feelings, so it worked. Honestly, I'm glad they both found someone who genuinely makes them happy."

Augusto placed his cup down and leaned forward, pressing his elbows into his knees. He thought about what she said and wondered what in the world made two people use each other for pleasure the way they had. How could you be intimate with someone with no emotional connection? Augusto rolled his shoulders. That was in Alex's past and he would be Alex's future. He licked his lips. "Be honest, you thought he was a little nuts when he told you about me. I mean come on, I shake my ass onstage to pay the bills."

"That's not why I thought he was crazy. I thought he was crazy because you two wanted to kill each other when you first met."

"Makes sense. I didn't like him—at all."

"He didn't like you either… until he saw you dance. That totally did it for him." She laughed. "Now he's head over heels."

Augusto laughed. "Did he tell you we had an argument that same night?"

"Sweetheart, he tells me everything."

"Everything?" Augusto questioned wide-eyed. Sure he told Keith everything but hearing a female knew about their sex life was a little strange to him. "As in *everything* everything?"

"E-ver-y-thing," she drawled, smirking as she looked him up

and down.

"Wow…." Augusto sipped his now lukewarm tea. "All of it, eh…"

Carolynne grinned triumphantly as she repositioned herself in the chair. She still wore that devious smile, like she knew every single secret Augusto and Alex had. He spent a moment weighing that fact, but the sound of the door opening behind them pulled him away from thoughts of what exactly Carolynne knew. Alex stood behind them, eyeing them both like they stole something.

"What's going on?" he asked.

"Oh, just chatting with your fiancé," Carolynne said with a wink in Augusto's direction.

"Oh, we're talking, all right," Augusto agreed and groaned when Alex sat across his lap. "There are some things you and I need to have a conversation about." He smiled.

"Is that so?" Alex leaned up to Augusto's ear, whispering so that his lips brushed his fiancé's jaw. "What do we need to talk about, lover?"

"Oh, man." Augusto shivered. "I can't remember."

"Carolynne, I think the boys need help cleaning up," Alex all but purred.

She gave him a sarcastic smile and pushed up from the chair, but before going back inside, she said, "Do what you want. I'll hear about it tomorrow." And she stuck her tongue out at them both.

Augusto moaned and pressed his face into Alex's chest. "Not cool, lover, not cool at all."

Alex laughed softly, running his fingers through Augusto's hair. "She's a brat. And I promise I won't tell her anything tomorrow." He lowered his voice. "She doesn't know half of what she thinks she knows."

"So she doesn't know about that thing I do with my tongue?" Augusto grinned, lifting his mouth to the side of Alex's head. He dropped a kiss there. "Or the way you come alive in my arms?"

He tugged lightly at Alex's ear. "I don't want her to know. I want her to wonder about the smile on your face every time she sees you."

"That'll be our little secret," Alex said in an airy rush. "How about we go to the bedroom and you make me come alive, lover?"

Augusto chuckled. "I'm not too full for that."

CHAPTER FORTY-ONE

"You're going to do me a favor," Alex said into the phone. He peeked out the door of his bedroom to make sure Keith was still occupied in the living room. Augusto had left for Santo's nearly an hour ago. And while this whole plan felt completely underhanded, Alex would do what he had to make sure his fiancé stayed in school.

"You're not going to say no either." Alex closed the door and locked it, then sat down on the edge of the bed he shared with the man he loved more than anything. "This is not negotiable."

"Not negotiable, huh? What exactly do you want from me, Alexander?" Ross asked, voice cool and condescending, only because Alex hadn't dropped the bomb on him yet.

"I want you to pay Augusto's tuition for the next two semesters."

"Who? What?"

"My fiancé. His tuition to Juilliard. Two semesters."

"And why would I do that?"

"Because if you don't, I'll tell your wife about our two year love affair and how we'd been fucking when you told her you never cheated on her. Then I'll tell my mother and father how you raped me."

"Raped? I never raped you!"

"Ross, I was seventeen years old. You're my father's age. That's statutory rape."

"Well...well, they won't do anything about it. Too much time has passed." Oh, how quickly Ross's tone changed. The man sounded terrified now. "That was a long time ago. You can't—"

"Do you think your wife will care how long ago it was? Do you think my parents will care?"

Silence.

Alex's throat tightened. Maybe this was a bad idea. Ross had been out of his life for years now. Why bring the asshole back into it? Especially now that things were better than Alex could've ever dreamed of.

"So, that's it?" Ross finally said. "You're going to blackmail me?"

"'Blackmail' is such a harsh word, don't you think?" Alex crossed his legs and sat back on his bed, utterly pleased with himself now that he knew Ross was shaking in his designer leather loafers. "So, are you going to pay the tuition or do I need to call your wife?"

"I want to see you, Alexander," Ross said. "You looked so handsome when I saw you last. All grown up. Debonair. Have lunch with me, or…or coffee."

"What part of 'my fiancé' didn't you understand? Besides, I don't even like you. I don't want to see you. Every time I think of you or hear someone say your name, bile rises up the back of my throat. I hate you, Ross."

"There's a thin line between love and—"

"Just stop."

Alex pushed up from the bed and started pacing the room. His blood was on the explosive side of boiling right now—an effect he swore he would never let the other man have on him again. He gripped the phone tight to his ear, trying like hell not to seethe because he didn't want to give the bastard the satisfaction.

He stopped pacing, exhaled slowly, smiled and said, "We will never, ever have anything to do with each other again. So you might as well get that thought out of your head. I don't want to see you at family gatherings. I don't want to see you anyway. Ever! You—for all I care—can eat shit and die. Now, unless you want your world rocked in a very, very bad way, I suggest you make a call to Juilliard and make a payment on Augusto Catalan's account, and it better be done tomorrow or I'm calling your wife."

Ross wasn't given a single second to argue or make lewd remarks. Alex hung up before Ross even finished taking the breath he'd tried to suck down. He pitched the phone onto the bed then flung himself down beside it.

Staring up at the ceiling, Alex silently prayed he hadn't just royally messed up. He hoped Augusto wouldn't get pissed off about this, but even if he did, at least he would be pissed off with two more semesters at Juilliard and his dreams even closer to happening. Alex wouldn't have done it if he thought the school and dancing meant nothing to Augusto, but it did. It meant the world to Augusto, and he had so much talent. Shame to see it go to waste.

CHAPTER FORTY-TWO

Walking into Santo's, Augusto forced himself to see his future running the place. With the way things were going that was the only alternative. He would have to make it even bigger than it currently stood since Alex was used to expensive things and he wanted to be able to provide for them. Still, he just couldn't see himself not on the stage for a very long time. What would happen if he dropped out of Julliard?

He would always be known as the man who dropped out of Julliard.

Leaning on the door frame, he didn't really feeling like speaking to anyone, but Luther called and asked for a meeting. The last thing he wanted to do was be out of bed, and if he had to be up, then he'd rather be lounging in the pool soothing his aching muscles. Final recitals were coming up for the term and his whole body ached since he was doing double time.

"I'm glad you came." Luther's voice pulled him away from his post and he turned. The older man passed by him and entered the rehearsal space, so Augusto followed. They didn't speak other than the one line and after Luther closed the door and Augusto sat on the floor beside the stool, he was basically waiting for Luther to say something. "This is not going to be an easy discussion."

Augusto's heart did a flip—was he being fired? Was he being forced to choose between Santo's and Julliard? Was his dancing not like it used to be? What was going on?

"Okay. Then do it like a Band-Aid."

Luther chuckled. "It's not that kind of hard, Gus. It's about Kemar. I know this is a weird time to bring it up but he asked me to do this once you were engaged or married to someone else."

"What?"

"Just listen for a sec." Luther took a breath, a low whoosh

sound and exhaled long and hard. "When Kemar realized he was about to die he did a few things. He got you that necklace and he spoke with me the morning before you came in. He explained his life insurance policy to me and told me I would get the money after his death. He also told me that since I didn't need the money I was supposed to give it to you once you got married."

"How did he know I would get married? I didn't want to. But then I met Alex and it just happened."

"Kemar didn't want you sitting around moping after he was gone. The money is to help you make a life for yourself and he knew if he'd told you about it you would be all macho and shit so—he did it this way."

Tears flowed down Augusto's cheeks then. So many emotions flowed through him. From relief to fear to sadness to the most profound happiness he could possibly imagine. Great things were happening for him and he just couldn't hold it all in anymore. He hadn't cried in years yet there he was, tears in his eyes because of everything happening.

That didn't last long, for a smile crossed his lips as he thought that Kemar was the one who'd made him come the closest to walking down the aisle, before Alex.

"Are you all right, son?"

Was he? Augusto wasn't sure. But he nodded. "This couldn't have come at a better time."

"What do you mean?"

"Tuition is due at Julliard—I got my final notice." He wiped his nose with the back of his hand and raked his hair back. "Alex was freaking out. I was trying not to lose it. I didn't know what I was going to do. I was figuring I'd drop out."

"Like hell. Not on my watch. You take this money and pay your tuition. I'll write you a check now then take it out of what I have for you from Kemar. How much do you owe?"

"I paid some of it. But I still owe them eight thousand."

"All right. I'll write you a check for that amount and since I know you won't take it as a gift, I'll subtract that from the two hundred thousand Kemar left you—deal?"

Augusto rose from where he was sitting and hugged Luther so tight the older man laughed and pushed at him.

"Sorry. I didn't mean to hold on so tight. But you and your marvelous son are saving my life."

§§§

Armed with the final notice and the check, Augusto went to pay the tuition. After giving his student number, he waited while the lady behind the counter tapped away at her keyboard.

"Hmm…" she said.

"Hmm? What does that mean?" Augusto asked.

"You don't owe the school anything for this semester," she explained.

Augusto arched a brow. "What? But I got this letter."

"I understand but see…" She turned the screen so he could see it from where he stood, and pointed to the records. "It says here you paid for not only this semester but the next."

"I didn't…" Realization surged through him and he shook his head. "Jesus…"

"Son, I'm sure He helped you with the money but I highly doubt He paid it. Now you must have forgotten you did."

"It's fine. I'll come back."

Walking away, Augusto searched for Alex at all his regular haunts. From Carolynne's place to a bunch of others until he found Alex sitting with some other dancers in a rehearsal room. Storming in, he ignored everyone else and glared at Alex. "We need to talk."

"I, um…" Alex frowned, looked at the group surrounding him and said, "Give me a minute," before pushing up from the floor. He padded across the room. Augusto immediately headed into the hall and Alex followed. "What's wrong?"

"When we had the argument about my tuition, I asked you to

leave it alone. Now I go to pay it and it's already paid?"

Alex sighed and leaned against the wall as if he'd expected this but wasn't ready to deal with it. "Your 'I'll figure it out' didn't inspire a lot of confidence, baby. I was scared and I reacted." Alex shrugged. "That's just how I am."

"Shit, Alex." Augusto dragged his fingers through his hair and turned away from him. Then another thought hit him. "You have to pay your parents back. I'll write you a check."

"No, the money doesn't have to be paid back and it won't be paid back," Alex said with absolute resolve.

"I don't want this on me, Alex. I especially don't want to owe your parents anything. I asked you not to get involved but as usual you go off halfcocked, completely ignoring what I said and do what you want anyway. Now, you're paying this money back to your parents or I will."

"Augusto," Alex said, resting a hand on Augusto's forearm and looking him right in the eyes. "Let it go, baby. Just take the money and forget about it, okay?"

Augusto shook his head and pushed Alex's arm from him. "You don't get it. After all this time you still don't understand me. I don't want your money. I'm going to write a check out to your parents and whether they are in the South of France or Timbuktu, I'm taking it to them. You had no right to make that decision for me."

Alex lowered his head and softly said, "It didn't come from my parents."

"What do you mean the money didn't…Alex…?" Augusto said in a way that spoke volumes of the quickly disappearing control he had on his temper. "Where did the money come from?"

At first, Alex didn't say anything. He only stood there with his head down and his foot beating uncontrollably against the floor. "Don't freak out, okay? Because whatever you might think, I didn't do anything for the money."

Augusto groaned. It was a sound he didn't mean to leave him but it happened and he couldn't take it back. Whenever someone prefaced something by saying don't freak out there was usually cause to freak out. With Alex don't freak out seemed to have a way of bashing him over the head with a resounding freak the fuck out!

"For fuck's sakes, Alex! The money—where did you get it?"

"Ross."

When Augusto was seventeen he was kicked in the stomach by a horse. He remembered falling to the ground, in so much pain he couldn't cry, scream or even think. The air had been knocked out of him and he'd merely curled into a ball clutching his stomach. That was the same feeling Augusto had now—without curling into a ball. Shaking his head, he swallowed the angry, disgusted lump that formed in his throat and took a step back.

"I can't talk to you right now," he managed.

"Don't do this to me. I saw your dreams crumbling and after what that asshole did to me, the least he could do was pay for your tuition."

"Don't do this to you? Hell, Alex this is not about you! You went behind my back and you took money, not from your parents, I could have gotten over that, but you went and you took money from him? You didn't think what that would do to me, did you? Did you!"

Augusto heard himself yelling, felt his body shaking with the fury of what was happening and what had happened. He stepped back with a hand held up. He meant to say something else but the words just wouldn't come. He took a breath and stalked off.

"Augusto, wait!" Alex yelled out, storming down the hall after him. Augusto heard the frantic footfalls, but didn't stop. "I didn't know what else to do," Alex admitted, voice quivering. "I had to do something. I couldn't watch you walk away from school. Please talk to me."

"You should have done what I asked," Augusto said simply. He stopped and turned in Alex's direction. A crowd was starting to gather along the hall, staring at the argument. But Augusto paid them no attention. "I don't know if I want to talk to you right now, Alex. I have to go."

When he turned back a few dancers were blocking his path so he shoved hard sending one toppling to the floor.

"Hey!" the other dancer shouted.

Instead of stopping, Augusto shoved his fingers into his pocket and took the stairs down to the ground floor. Once there, he wasn't sure what to do with himself. He just couldn't stop shaking.

CHAPTER FORTY-THREE

Eyes burning, heart slowly dying, Alex watched Augusto walk away, wanting nothing more than to run after his man and beg him not to be pissed off. It wouldn't do any good though, and Alex knew that. Despite what Augusto thought, Alex knew him well. Alex had messed up thinking he could fix something for Augusto without him getting this upset. Augusto was way too proud for that.

Alex stumbled backward. Everyone kept staring, some with genuine concern and sympathy, some with triumph because the mighty had finally fallen. Oh, how the mighty had truly fallen. None of them mattered right now though, because the only person Alex cared about had just stormed away from him.

He turned and ran the opposite way down the hall, cleared the stairs and slammed through the front doors. The cold winter air felt like pins and needles pushing against his tear-moistened cheeks. He doubled over and gripped his knees, fighting to suck in as much icy wind as he could. It didn't help. He still couldn't breathe and his heart now frantically pounded, as though it were trying to make up for the beats it had missed while Alex fought to keep Augusto from leaving him behind.

"Taxi!" he thrust his arm into the air and started waving.

From the school, he could've walked to his parents' Manhattan home, but he didn't trust his legs to make the three mile walk, and he had to get the hell away from there now. The other students' staring eyes and gaping mouths were now seared into his head, and though he could feel all his hard won power quickly fading, it didn't seem to matter as much because Augusto had walked away from him.

"Munsey Park. Quickly," Alex panted, settling into the backseat.

The cab jostled Alex as it pulled away from the curb. He laid his head back against the seat and closed his eyes. It felt like at any second he would lose the brown rice and steamed veggies he'd had for lunch.

With traffic, it took more than an hour to get to his parents' multi-million dollar colonial nestled in the middle of upper class suburbia. He told the driver where and when to turn, and when the big white façade of his boyhood home came into view, his stomach only tightened worse.

"This is it," he said and the cab pulled to a stop.

Alex handed over a wad of uncounted cash then lazily carried himself up to the service entrance on the side of the house. Every time he'd ever snuck out, that was the way he'd always returned. The maids and butler, the groundskeepers and whoever the hell else his father kept on payroll didn't give a damn about Alex's comings and goings, as long as it didn't interfere with their work or piss Mr. Benton off enough to take his anger out on them.

As soon as he slipped inside the door, all movement stopped. They stared as he trudged through the kitchen and up the hidden set of stairs at the back of the house. He padded down the hall to his old bedroom then sank down on the edge of the bed.

And that's when Alex truly fell apart.

Hands covering his face, his shoulders shook as he sobbed uncontrollably. In all the time he'd been with Augusto, he'd never felt so lost and scared. He'd never felt like the entire world was being pulled out from under him. In fact, Augusto gave him the entire world and then some, but now…

"I'm so sorry," he cried out to no one. "I didn't know what to do."

Something stupid caught his eye, the only gift or sign of pride his father had ever given him and it hadn't even been after doing something huge like graduating high school or getting into Juilliard. It had been a reward for something stupid, catching a glitch in the company accounting that was costing his father a whole thirty-five thousand and some change a year. It was a golden Rolex with a single tiny diamond in the face, and so fucking tacky Alex had refused to wear it.

The watch pissed him off. It represented everything that was wrong with Alex, why he didn't deserve to be loved by someone as wonderful as Augusto, why he didn't deserve to be a part of the Catalan family, why he'd made the dumbass mistake of calling Ross to get Augusto's tuition paid for instead of trusting his fiancé like he'd asked.

He pushed himself up from the bed, picked the watch up and eyed it for a long moment. Money. Everything came down to money. That was the lesson of his childhood. Broken love could be fixed with an expensive gift. Friendships could be saved with a sizeable chunk of change. Kids could raise themselves with the best toys and a few well-paid nannies. And that was the reason Alex didn't know how to function in a relationship like the one he had with Augusto. Ross had pacified him with fine food and designer clothes, trips and expensive toys. Ross had pacified him with sex and promises. Augusto genuinely loved him, and because of the unfamiliarity of genuine love, Alex only knew how to screw it up.

He swiped the watch from the desk it had been sitting on for the last seven or so years, staring at it for a long time, taking in everything that hunk of metal and gadgetry represented to him. He let it consume him and fill him so he would never forget how money and frivolous things had a way of tearing down everything beautiful and holy in the world. Alex slammed the watch down on the hardwood floor, reached for the bat beside his desk and started swinging. He beat every ounce of anger and disappointment in himself into that watch, and didn't stop until every bone and muscle in his body ached.

By the time he stopped, he was so winded, the air in his lungs was on fire and his pulse raced so fast it felt like it would blow out a vein. The adrenaline pumping through him made his stomach ache, and the rage made him want to keep going. He couldn't do it though. It hurt too badly and all he wanted was to be with Augusto again. Now, the anger and disappointment with himself became true hurt.

Alex stumbled back to his bed, curled in a fetal ball around the many pillows at his headboard, and lay there completely spent of energy and tears, drained of emotion and will. He stared at the wall until the plaid pattern became a blur and the light overhead turned dark.

CHAPTER FORTY-FOUR

"I wasn't expecting you tonight," his mother said. "Don't you have classes tomorrow?"

Augusto made a face, hugged her then slumped into a nearby chair. "I don't know about Alex and I, Mammie."

"You just asked him to marry you. How can you not be sure?"

"It's not that I don't love him. I do. I was short on tuition, he found out and did the same stupid thing he always does."

"And that is?"

"Stuck his nose in and ruined everything."

"But he loves you, Gus."

Augusto winced. "Don't say that right now."

"What precisely did he do?" she walked over to sit across from him and caressed his hand gently. "What did he do that was so bad?"

"When he was younger he had...relations...with a man—a very older—very married—man. He paid my tuition for two semesters but he took it from this person. When I thought the money came from his parents I was upset but I could have overlooked it and just paid them back. To find out it came from that man just made me so furious..."

"I understand why you are furious, son. But do you know how hard it must have been for him to go back to an ex on your behalf?"

"Don't call him an ex—he's a rapist—Alex was a child!"

"Oh my."

They went silent and Augusto pulled his hand away from his mother. He rose and grabbed a large jug of juice from the fridge and a couple of glasses. When he sat again, he took a breath and forgot the juice was there so his mother poured it.

"I don't know why he believes money can fix everything, Mammie. Your heart is broken—buy a gift. Your world is falling apart—give money. No puedo vivir así. I can't live like this, Mammie. What am I going to do?"

"I didn't raise you to let money consume you, Gus. But you can either break up with him or you can speak with him about it. Either way, something has to give."

"I don't want to break up. I just—damn, why is this so hard?"

"Love is always hard. The ones worth fighting for are a royal pain in the behind. But think about it—Alex faced a demon for you."

"I thought about that. I know I have the necklace from Kemar but Kemar loved me—truly loved me. That man didn't care enough to wait a year until Alex turned eighteen. How am I supposed to feel knowing that man violated the man I love and now he's paying for a dream that used to be so pure for me? It's tainted now."

"Is that why you're not going to school tomorrow? Because you think your dream is tainted?"

Augusto said nothing. His mother's words were a little truer than he cared to admit.

"Hijo, escúchame." His mother's index finger went up and her neck glided dramatically to one side. "You're not letting this ruin your chances of graduating from that school. Do you know how many doors this could open up for you? If it'll help, pay the money back and carry on. I know you said Kemar left you some so use it. As for Alex, it's just what I said before. Either talk to him or let him go. You can't have it both ways."

"He didn't come home last night."

"See?"

Augusto made a face. He wasn't even sure why he came to New Jersey to talk to his mother about his dating life. She was too practical. He kissed her cheek. "I love you, Mammie."

"Where are you going?"

"I don't know."

Outside the air was frigid. He never liked the snow and thankfully it seemed to be melting. He grabbed his cell and called Keith.

"Hey, Keith, can you do me a favor?"

"Sure, what's wrong?"

"I'm trying to find someone…"

"Gus…I'd have to call my buddy down at the station. But sure. Who?"

"Ross Emerson."

"Oh dude, you don't need the cops for that. Just go to his website. He's some top-shit businessman of sorts. Why don't you come home and I'll get you the information?"

"All right. See you in a bit."

Going home took a little longer and by the time he did manage to get there, he was practically frozen. Still he got the address from Keith and spent the night with his guitar in his lap on his bed.

Once again, Alex didn't come home.

"I know you didn't check in on him because you're angry," Keith said, walking into the room and sitting at the foot of the bed. "So I did."

"Is he okay?"

"He's fine. My buddy said he's at his family's place. Gus, you should talk to him."

Augusto didn't reply. He strummed the strings before putting the guitar on the floor. "Sorry I woke you up," he said simply before rolling over to his side.

He listened to Keith's footsteps leaving the room and closed his eyes.

Bright and early the next morning, Augusto went from Luther's place to the bank. When he had a small bag with cash in it, the amount it cost for his two semesters of tuition, he got into a cab and headed to Ross's place. Ringing the doorbell brought unbearable anger to the forefront of Augusto's heart and he tapped his foot uncontrollably on the expensive rock lining the porch.

Ross's wife opened the door with bright eyes and a smile. "I remember you! Augusto, right? Alex's mother told me you are engaged to Alex, congratulations!"

"Where is your husband?"

"Ross? He's in the den…"

"Take me to him."

The smile was gone from her face. He could tell she wanted to ask but didn't. Silently, he followed her to where Ross was seated. He jerked to his feet the moment he laid eyes on Augusto. Without waiting to be announced, Augusto stepped fully around the woman and chucked the bag at Ross who caught it heavily into his chest.

"Here's your money!" Augusto snapped. "I don't want shit from you."

"Money for what?" his wife asked.

Ross spluttered.

"Ask your husband…and by the way, Ross, know this. If it was up to me, I'd put my foot so far up your ass you would be able to taste the dirt on the bottom of my shoe. But Alex is a lot more forgiving than I am."

"Ross? What's he talking about?"

Augusto continued as though she hadn't spoken. "Come near Alexander again and I will personally break every bone in your dishonest, pathetic body—got that?"

Ross looked back and forth between Augusto and a very impatiently curious Mrs. Emerson.

"I'll ask you one more time," she said, arms crossing her chest. "What the hell is he talking about?"

"I…I…" Ross stammered.

"What? Now you're speechless?" Augusto frowned.

"I think you have me confused, kid," Ross said, maneuvering his way past Augusto.

Augusto grabbed his arm and yanked him back into the room. He was going to walk away but this miserable excuse of a man just really irritated him.

"Maybe I should call the cops," Marilynn said.

"Oh, actually, that would be great," Augusto spat. "Because by the end, we'll be picking up what's left of Ross' reputation from all over the New York city area. And I have you confused? You think I'm a kid? Well, when Alexander was seventeen your amazing husband seduced him and had sex with him…"

She gasped.

"Repeatedly. Alex thought they were in a relationship but it was all a joke to you, wasn't it, Ross? From where I'm standing, I'm more of man than you will ever be!"

"Lies! All lies!" Ross insisted.

"Lies?" Augusto clenched his fists by his sides and took a step toward Ross. He wasn't sure what Marilynn was thinking but she stepped between them and rested a hand to Augusto's chest. Augusto looked at the woman with his head tilted.

"If you hit him," she said, voice soft and even. "He'll have his greedy team of lawyers on you faster than you can blink. You go home and send my apologies to Alex. Ross won't be a problem anymore, I assure you."

Her eyes were generous and kind, Augusto wondered how such a woman could be with a man like Ross. Then her eyes changed to those of a woman with a plan and he was glad he wouldn't be on the receiving end of what she had in mind.

Glaring at Ross one final time, Augusto thanked her and walked from the house feeling lighter. For the first time since she'd said it, he realized it wasn't the threat of lawyers he was scared of. It was Alex seeing him as anything but what he was. He didn't like fighting but he could sure carry his own and with what Ross did to Alex, he wouldn't have felt bad about it.

He hopped into another cab, this time, heading to Alex's place.

CHAPTER FORTY-FIVE

It had been two days since Alex had slept in his own bed, with the man who consumed his thoughts and his life. Two long, painful days since he'd kissed Augusto and held him through the night. And now it was time to go home and make amends or throw in the towel and call it quits.

He hefted a backpack of things he wanted to keep onto his shoulders and headed out the service entrance. A black sedan was supposed to be waiting in the driveway, but when Alex raised his head, he found Augusto leaning against a yellow cab.

Alex gasped, both hands shooting up to his mouth. The urge to run across the pavement and throw himself at his fiancé made him tremble where he stood.

Somehow he managed to take a few steps forward. He said, "Please, don't tell me you're here to break up with me."

"You see that's your problem. You always jump to the wrong conclusion."

"Augusto," Alex said, tightening his arms around his own chest. He drew in a deep breath, then very slowly let it go. "I'm about as imperfect as they come. I don't know how to do relationships because I've never even had the most basic, most unconditional relationship with anyone. I make bad decisions with the best intentions. That's what I am. I'm sorry if that disappoints you. I love you, but that's the truth of what I am."

"You have to start listening to me, Alex. That's all I ask. This is partially my fault because I'm so used to dealing with my issues alone. I'm used to fending for myself but you can't just throw money at everything—well, except Ross's head with a really big bag."

"What?" Alex frowned. "You had me until Ross's head."

"I gave him his money back," Augusto replied, unfolding his arms and pushing his hands into his pockets. "I told him if he came anywhere near you again I'd break him. I meant it."

"Wow. That's better than I could've done." Alex looked down again, kicking his shoe over the pavement. Without lifting his head again, he said, "I've missed you."

"Alex, come here."

Alex took a few carefully laid steps closer, wishing like hell he had it in him to reach out and grab Augusto into a hug. He slowly looked up, but didn't raise his chin. "Yeah?"

Augusto didn't speak. He merely reached out, hooked his fingers behind Alex's neck and pulled him forward. Alex crashed into his chest and without time to breathe, his mouth was captured in a raw kiss.

Alex melted into the kiss, and the press of their bodies and the hope that came with finally having Augusto hold him again. He gripped his boyfriend's hips and when Augusto pulled back, Alex had to fight not to whimper in protest.

"We can't do this again," Augusto whispered. "I don't do well without you."

"You don't?" Alex laughed. "You should see the Rolex my father gave me." Augusto frowned. Alex shook his head. "It's not important. I love you so much. I swear to God it felt like half of my soul was missing."

"I love you, too," Augusto replied. "Can we go home now?"

"God, please," Alex said with a smile. "I miss my own bed almost as much as I miss sleeping in your arms."

Augusto smiled and kissed him again. "Okay. Let's go home. I can make you some dinner and we can just relax a little."

"I love that plan."

Alex swung his gaze from the cab on the curb and the sedan in the driveway, realizing he was at one of those crossroads where he always seemed to make a wrong turn with respect to Augusto. Alex would've normally jumped at the chance to pay for anything Augusto needed and apparently, that was a major part of their problems.

"Since we'll get more privacy in the sedan," he said, looking back at Augusto, "why don't you pay for the cab and we'll take the sedan into the city?"

Augusto nodded and walked off to the cab. Alex watched him have a small conversation with the cab driver before Augusto laughed at something the man said. Money was exchanged and Augusto reached in and bumped fists with the driver. When he came back he was smiling. "I think you sent my car away so you could have your way with this body."

"Mmm…you know me so well," Alex said as he hooked his hand around Augusto's waistband. He tugged him closer and nipped the edge of his lover's chin. "It's been awhile since I've touched you, baby. I think I should get all the intimate time I want." He smirked, teasing Augusto with his stare.

"I know you're messing with me," Augusto whispered, turning his head to drag his lips over the side of Alex's face. "But I will let you since I don't have class or work anytime soon."

"So, does that mean I get you all to myself until morning? Or maybe we can just stay in bed all day."

"It all depends," Augusto said softly. "What's it worth to you?"

"If I could give you the world, that would be but a fraction of your worth to me."

"See? That's just it. I don't want the world. I just…I want you." Augusto punctuated his words by kissing Alex's nose and pulling him into the car.

In the car, the first thing Alex did was put up the privacy wall. The driver already knew exactly where to go, and Alex didn't want to waste a single second with the man of his dreams. "I only want you, too," Alex said, "for the record." And that was the absolute truth. All the money in the world wouldn't make him happy if he didn't have Augusto. He could honestly say that because he'd always had everything he'd wanted—an infinite supply of funds and anything he could dream of—but he didn't know real happiness until Augusto danced into his life.

CHAPTER FORTY-SIX

Augusto pulled Alex into his lap, legs bracing astride his just to feel the heat of his lover's body. Taking Alex's lips in a real kiss after so long left him feeling hungry and wanting. He fed from his lover's mouth, remembering just how much he loved to kiss his man. A raw sound he couldn't control escaped his throat even as he deepened the kiss while caressing the back of Alex's neck. His free hand was busy fondling Alex's ass, memorizing the tightness of it, the beauty of it. Groaning, he slipped that hand into the back of Alex's pants, feeling out the crack and tracing it lightly with the tips of his fingers.

The only reason he finally wrenched his mouth away was to breathe, to remember his lungs needed air. Panting, he pressed his forehead into Alex's shoulder. He whispered his love repeatedly for he just couldn't control it. Once it was out, the words continued spilling from his lips.

He felt Alex's warm breath weave around his earlobe, just before he heard Alex say, "I'm all yours, baby. I love only you."

His body trembled hearing Alex's words and feeling his lover's lips against his ear. He gripped Alex's hips and pushed down, forcing his fiancé's ass to grind into his cock. Augusto gasped, mouth opened, seeking out the soft spot between Alex's neck and shoulder. Augusto sucked at it before grazing the flesh with his teeth even as his hips worked upward, pressing his clothed dick into the covered crevice of Alex's ass.

"You're such a tease," Alex breathed, reaching down between their bodies to grip Augusto's cock. "You know it'll take an hour to get back to Manhattan from here. We have…time."

"Don't you feel that?" Augusto questioned. "Do you seriously think I can hold out for an hour?"

"Mmm…"

As Augusto continued nipping at Alex's neck, Alex fought

zipper and fabric to free Augusto's cock. It took Augusto lifting his hips—which pushed his erection harder against Alex's ass—before Alex could get his pants down far enough to completely free Augusto.

"I want you. Now," Alex said, rubbing his palm over Augusto's naked shaft.

"I didn't bring anything with me," Augusto grunted.

"I, um…I don't have anything either." Alex stilled. "I stopped carrying condoms in my wallet when we started dating."

"Why is that? Didn't you think we would be in the backseat of a car needing one?" Augusto questioned. He tried hiding his mirth but failed miserably.

Alex rolled his eyes. "No, I suppose I didn't. I just knew I didn't need them because I didn't want anyone else. But back to the problem at hand…what do you want to do about it?"

Augusto pouted up at his darling. "We could stop somewhere. I'm sure there are stores around—somewhere."

He wasn't really paying attention at this point. Both his hands were in Alex's pants, fondling, feeling for his hole and caressing slightly. Those lips he loved sucking on so much parted and Alex's tongue flowed over them. But Augusto wanted more. Sliding Alex from his lap, he motioned to the back seat. "I want you to kneel, face the outside and spread your legs."

"Shit," Alex breathed, without hesitating for a single second. He climbed up onto the seat and buried his face in the leather, ass in the air, ready and willing.

For a moment, Augusto merely pressed his back into the divider and watched Alex. Finally, he reached in and caressed a hand down the small of Alex's back, over the rise of his ass and down his thigh. Gripping both sides of Alex's pants, Augusto braced himself, dug his fingers in and pulled. The sheer sound of material coming apart echoed through the car. Having Alex take his pants off would've taken too long. The same was done to his boxers and soon Alex's rounded ass was arched perfectly for his taking. A smile washed over his face as he leaned forward, spread those beautiful cheeks and delved in with his tongue.

"Oh. Damn. Ah," Alex rasped, throwing his head back. He reached for Augusto with one hand, leaving the other to hold him in place, but barely managed to graze Augusto's hair. "Dear, God, don't stop."

Augusto took Alex's hand from his head and restrained it by his side. He used his free hand to spread Alex's cheeks and licked deeper. Each sound or word from his lover was used as an encouragement to drill his tongue deeper. Augusto sucked on a finger and inserted it in to the first knuckle. "Is this what you wanted, Alex?" Augusto asked, withdrawing the finger, sucking it wet and pressing it back into him.

"Not. Exactly." By the sound of Alex's voice, he had his jaw clenched tight, and when Augusto slipped the second finger in, Alex pushed a hard breath through his lips. "I. Want. Your. Cock."

"Not like this. I could hurt you."

"Shit," Alex breathed, dropping his head lower. From where Augusto kneeled, he could see the slow rise and fall of Alex's chest, the rounding of his shoulders and the way he was suddenly so relaxed.

"Alex…" The name tumbled like a prayer from Augusto's lips. The car went over a slight bump and he gripped Alex's shoulder. His fingers slipped deeper. "Damn—I'm trying to be a gentleman here and you're not making it easy."

"I'm sorry, I just…" Alex shifted his hips back, forcing Augusto's digits to dip further. A groan left Alex's lips, followed by a quick shiver. "Like I said, I missed you."

Stripping in the back seat of a car wasn't easy, even in a luxury car. With a few bumps and groans, Augusto managed to pull himself up high enough to get his cock lathered in saliva and aimed at Alex's entrance. He slipped the head in and his knees went weak, sending him flopping slightly over Alex's body. Alex's channel squeezed him sweetly, burning him so good. "I want you to take me when you can," Augusto whispered, caressing down

Alex's back. "This is all up to you."

From behind, he watched the back of Alex's head slowly bobbing up and down. He saw the way Alex's chest expanded as he kept his breathing nice and even.

"I love you," Alex whispered.

Augusto gained an inch, maybe two. Alex breathed again, leaning more into it now. After another deep breath and a hiss, Augusto was buried to the hilt and his fiancé's muscled walls gripped him tight.

"Just go slow," Alex whispered. "Everything's fine."

They took it inch by painstaking inch until his hips met Alex's cheeks. A whimper echoed from Augusto's body but he didn't care. Alex had a way of doing that to him, taking all his control and turning his very being upside down. With his eyes closed, he pulled all the way back out except for the head, licked at his palm and slathered the exposed area of his cock. A few more times and he was working into Alex, freely, grinding like a dance that left them moving in unison against each other. The leather creaked as Alex's fingers and Augusto's knees dug into it. The car hit another bump which pushed Augusto deeper into his fiancé.

"Oh shit!" Augusto cried before biting his lower lip. "You drive me...crazy."

"Crazy." Alex took a minute to catch his breath. "Yeah. Crazy. Good."

Leaning forward, Augusto licked at the spot between Alex's shoulders. He sucked the flesh into his mouth then blew against it. He dragged his day-old beard against Alex's flesh, enjoying the feel of Alex's body working beneath him.

"Augusto," Alex whispered.

Augusto replied but not in words. Instead, he drove into his lover harder. Alex was loosened now and could take a nice, steady pounding. Bracing his arms on either side of Alex's body, Augusto pushed to the tips of his toe and rose up as much as the limited space would let him. It was amazing how good being with

Alex again felt. It was like the first cup of coffee in the morning as that heat flowed within him, spreading warmth to every inch of him. Augusto wasn't sure but he knew if he kept going the way he was he'd be blissfully burned alive and there was nothing he wanted more.

The next summer

Augusto was still tired. He'd spent the whole weekend filling in at Santo's for Chet, who'd taken off to some island with a new man. He was over the moon for his friend, but that left Augusto with very little time to spend with Alex and working more than he really should be working with Julliard. Luther took pity on him and allowed him to only do half the shows Chet should have been doing and cancelled most of the others.

He yawned and caught the fruit Donny threw at him. He tossed the cantaloupe across to Jason, who caught it without a problem then stacked it with the others. Summer was finally here and Mammie was cooking all her boys a lovely dinner where they could sit around, talk and be general pains in her butt. Those dinners always did his heart well, especially after a long month. Jason was heading back to Japan for a few weeks and Augusto still hadn't discussed what he was going to do with Alex yet. The thought of going to visit Jason in Japan had crossed his mind but it was just a mere inkling of a thought.

"Hey, lover boy!" Donny called. "Pay attention! You're slowing down the line!"

Augusto turned in time to catch the fruit and tossed it to Jason who was laughing so hard he almost toppled over. "Keep your pants on," Augusto muttered. "I wasn't thinking about Alex that time."

"Where's Keith?" Jason questioned.

"He is doing some stuff at the Academy today then a test," Augusto replied. "He's coming up to his final stretch and he's over the moon but tired."

"I can understand that," Donny chimed in. "The Academy is no joke—especially for New York's finest."

Once the fruits were finished being stacked, Jason went about peeling and Augusto sliced and stacked them into two big bowls on the tables set up in the large backyard. He left Jason with Donny and entered the house to see if Mammie needed any help.

"Put seasoning on the cut up chicken for me and then stack the pieces on the barbecue," Mammie instructed.

"Sure," Augusto replied and set to work.

"Que paso?" Mammie questioned.

"What makes you think something is wrong?" Augusto asked.

"Por favor, hijo! I am your mother. I know these things. You're not having second thoughts about Alex, are you?"

"No. I just—it's taking too long to be his husband."

Mammie grinned. "Well, everything that's worth having takes time. You know that better than I do. I haven't told you how proud I am you two are waiting until after school is over to get married."

Augusto grinned. "I know. Planning a wedding takes time and with school and Santo's the thought of adding to all that right now terrifies us. Besides, we want to travel and do some stuff first. But we will get married."

"When your father and I met, we had no money at all," Mammie said. "Did I tell you how we got married?"

"No. How?"

His mother smiled and took a deep breath. She stuck her hand into a bowl with peas and water. "We had nothing but this house," she explained. "And the only reason we had this house was the man your father was working for gave it to us as present. We got married in the backyard, with the preacher from my church and two of my church sisters."

Augusto kissed the side of his mother's head just as a car pulled into the driveway.

"I thought all your friends were out back."

"Alex isn't here yet," Augusto replied. "And Keith is still in the city."

"Oh. All right." Mammie nodded. "Go see who that is."

"I'll give this to Donny to put on the grill in the meantime." Augusto carried the large bowl with raw meat to his brother before walking back through the house to the front door.

Augusto wrenched open the door in time catch Alex with his arm raised and his fist ready to knock. Alex smiled as soon as their eyes met.

"I'm so sorry," he said. "I meant to be here sooner, but Mom and Dad were going nuts trying to get ready for their cruise. I don't understand them. They're in town two days and…" Augusto arched a brow. "Sorry, it's been a crazy day and I'm rambling."

"Are you sure they are okay with this?" Augusto arched a brow. "I mean I'm not complaining, but it's like they don't want to meet me or something."

"Baby." Alex stepped through the door and right up to Augusto, both hands on his cheeks. "It's not you. Sometimes, I think they don't want to be anywhere near me. You remember when I said we came from very different worlds and having a tight family like you do was foreign to me?" Augusto nodded. "Well, now you see what I meant. I had a closer relationship with my nanny than I did with Mom."

Augusto kissed him. "Come on in. The guys are in the backyard. Mammie's in the kitchen."

Hand in hand, Augusto guided his fiancé through the house and into the kitchen where his mother was still working to prepare their meal. She stood at the sink, drying her hands, but as soon as the floor creaked under Augusto and Alex's footfalls, she raised her head.

"Hijo," she squealed, raising her hand to touch Alex's face. She kissed one cheek, then the other.

Augusto laughed. "Wait a second! You never greet me like that!"

"Aw, baby," Alex said, mocking with a pouty face.

His mother chuckled.

"You can make it up to me tonight." Augusto kissed Alex after smirking at him. He then turned to his mother. "And you… well, I think I see a carrot cake in my future?"

She laughed. "You cheated!"

"Did not!" Augusto protested, peeking over her shoulder. "Mmm, carrot cake!"

Mammie chuckled and pushed both him and Alex gently toward the exit. "You two git! You're cramping my style and killing my surprises."

"Come on, Alex. I can see when we're not wanted," Augusto teased, taking Alex's hand. He led him through the house, up a couple of stairs and out into the section of the house he and Donny had built on for his mother to read. It was a room that was flooded with light in the day. A hammock sat off to the side.

"This is my favorite room in the house," Augusto said needlessly, falling into the sofa.

"It's beautiful in here," Alex said. He stepped up to Augusto, wedging himself between Augusto's widely opened legs. He brushed his hand over his fiancé's hair. "I love you, and your family is…amazing. Your mom makes me feel so welcome here."

"That's because she sees how much I adore you." Augusto moaned and closed his eyes to enjoy Alex's touch. "She's come a long way. She was shocked when I told her I was gay."

"Wow. Really?" Alex frowned. "I can't imagine her not taking it well."

"She didn't yell and scream. I think she was just disappointed. I was supposed to get married to a female, have babies so she can shower them with sugar."

"Just because you're not straight doesn't mean she can't have grandkids, you know?"

He opened his eyes to look up into Alex's face. "I know that. She knows that. It's always the knee jerk reaction when mothers find out their sons are gay. And besides, she has Donny too so I don't think she's worried." He tilted his head then and met Alex's eyes for a long, silent moment. "Wait—you wanna be my baby daddy?"

Alex laughed so hard his shoulders shook. Then he leaned down and kissed Augusto's forehead. "I don't know. Maybe. One day. This whole family thing"—he waved his hand in a circular motion—"is kinda nice. It's one of those 'you don't realize what you're missing until someone shows you' type things, you know?"

"I know, baby. But we'd make a good family. We would have to. If we didn't Mammie would kick both our asses. Don't let the age on her fool you. She's strong."

Chuckling again, Alex sat down beside him, draping both legs over Augusto's knee as he laid his head back against the pillow. "You're going to have to play Santa Claus at Christmas. I'm just not that jolly."

"Hey, nerd boy. Are you calling me fat? Because jolly is always another word for fat."

"You?" Alex poked at his side. "Hell no, baby. You have the body of a god."

Augusto laughed softly. He pressed his palm to Alex's chest and caressed gently. "I'd love to be your Santa Claus, Alex, for you and our kids. But you're going to have to pay me."

"Mmm…paying you always ends well for me." Alex leaned up and nipped Augusto's bottom lip.

"Well, sweetie, I think we have a deal." Augusto moaned, wrapping his fingers around the back of Alex's neck to keep him close.

"Have I said I love you lately?" Alex's voice came out surprisingly husky.

Augusto groaned, wrapping an arm around his fiancé's hips and pulling him into his lap. "Not in the last little bit. I love you so completely. I will never get tired of hearing you say it."

"And I'll never stop saying it, lover," Alex whispered before lowering his lips to meet Augusto's.

Someone cleared their throat but Augusto was in too deep. He had Alex's body pressed into his and their tongues tangled with each other's. His heart was racing and all he wanted to do was get lost in his lover's body. Instead he pulled his mouth from Alex's and glanced around Alex's body.

"Donny, your timing stinks," Augusto groaned.

"My bad. You two wanna get a room already?" Donny smirked.

Augusto grabbed a cushion from the sofa and hurled it at his brother who merely laughed harder. "Wrap it up you two— Mammie needs you."

"Damn—hold this thought for later?" Augusto asked Alex.

Sighing, Alex climbed out of Augusto's lap and offered a hand. "Soon as we get home, you're mine."

ABOUT THE AUTHORS

ALLISON –

It all started with a dream that made her heart wrench and a set of mesmerizing eyes that begged to be seen, and Allison Cassatta the writer was born. A techie by trade, the day-dreamer in her wanted to sail away from the mundane, while the hopeless romantic in her searched for the perfect love story. Many poems and short stories were written before her first attempt at a novel and once that piece of her soul spilled onto paper, there was no stopping it.

She has an eye for the visually stunning and a mind that screams to bring that beauty to life. She gives her readers something they can feel in the depth of their heart, creates worlds they can touch and characters that become your best friend or worst enemy.

Born and raised in Memphis, Tennessee, big-city life was a rat-race that kept her busy in her career. It took moving with her new husband to a sleepy Mississippi town to make her realize that dreams can come true, and did they ever. She found herself a published author. She found her perfect romance.

Allison's accolades include 2013 Top Pick of the Year from The Novel Approach, 2013 All Romance Ebooks Bestseller, 2012 Rainbow Book Awards Honorable Mention Winner, 2011 Best-selling Author, 2011 Best Anthology. She is currently published with Dreamspinner Press, Silver Publishing, Amber Quill Press and MLR Press.

You can find more of her works by visiting www.allisoncassatta. com

REMMY —

Born as the middle child of five in Lawrence Tavern Jamaica, Remmy Duchene now lives in the cold, white north. When not writing, you can find Remmy pretending to be a photographer, cooking, spending bucket loads of time with family, taking courses online and working a day job. You can find Remmy Duchene online at www.remmyduchene.com and on twitter @ remmyduchene

TRADEMARKS ACKNOWLEDGMENT

CPSIA information can be obtained at www.ICGtesting.com
Printed in the USA
BVOW02s1404310314

349299BV00001B/13/P